Little Freddie's LEGACY

Little Freddie's LEGACY

KATHRYN COCQUYT

ILLUSTRATED BY
SYLVIA CORBETT

PELICAN PUBLISHING COMPANY
Gretna 1994

*The word "pelican" and the depiction of a pelican are
trademarks of Pelican Publishing Company, Inc., and are
registered in the U.S. Patent and Trademark office.*

Library of Congress Cataloging-in-Publication Data

Cocquyt, Kathryn.
    Little Freddie's legacy / Kathryn Cocquyt ; illustrated by Sylvia
Corbett.
        p.   cm.
    Summary: Recently retired racing champion Little Freddie finds a
mate in the blind Rosie, and they produce a filly who becomes a
champion in Ireland.
    ISBN 1-56554-000-X
    1. Horses—Juvenile fiction. [1. Horses—Fiction. 2. Horse
racing—Fiction.] I. Corbett, Sylvia, ill. II. Title.
PZ10.3.C645Lk 1994
[Fic]—dc20   93-5558
                                              CIP
                                              AC

*The words "Churchill Downs" and "Kentucky Derby" and the replication
of the "Twin Spires" are registered trademarks of Churchill Downs, Inc.,
and are used herein with the permission of Churchill Downs.*

Manufactured in the United States of America
Published by Pelican Publishing Company, Inc.
1101 Monroe Street, Gretna, Louisiana 70053

To Freddie
—K.C.
To the spirit from which all inspiration comes
—S.C.

Contents

Little Freddie's LEGACY

CHAPTER ONE

The Champion Retires

IT WAS THE MORNING after Christmas when Freddie walked out into the brisk winter air and saw a charcoal grey horse in the paddock next to his. It had snowed the night before, so there was a blanket of white on the ground that crunched beneath him as he moved, leaving shadowy impressions of his hooves. The trees were stripped of their leaves, and their branches appeared like the bony fingers of an aged human hand stretching to the clouds. There were dark patches on their trunks, where a deer had peeled away the bark.

Stopping a moment, Freddie flared his nostrils and inhaled the strong aroma of the wood burning in the fireplace as it drifted over from the main house. The red brick chimney puffed out a steady stream of smoke, and the colonial-style home, which had been filled with the sounds of people laughing and singing Christmas carols only the day before, sat quietly against the wintery backdrop. It seemed such a happy occasion for all of them, and they were all so nice when they came to his stall to visit him. One young girl even gave him a candy cane. How Freddie loved the gleam in their eyes as they

11

looked at him and proudly commented on the recently retired racing champion. He listened attentively to their recollections of his races, and he especially liked it when they recounted his Kentucky Derby victory.

"That was one of the most exciting races I have ever seen," one of them said as he patted Freddie on the neck.

"Sure was," the farm owner agreed, "but he's just another horse now. He'll have to prove himself here just like every other sire. I only hope his kids are as good as he was."

Recalling the excitement of his days as a racer, Freddie let out a blissful neigh. Kicking out his back legs once, he began to prance along the four-board fence of his paddock. He thought of the many mornings when he trained in weather just like this. It was so cold that steam would rise up from him as he sweat, and his warm breath would form a foglike cloud in front of him. He truly missed seeing the horses that trained with him, but in the midst of his reminiscing he suddenly realized that he had not yet greeted his new neighbor.

"Hey, you there," he called, stopping abruptly and facing the other horse. "Good morning!"

The horse did not move. It stood in the far corner with its back to the chestnut thoroughbred, acting as if it had not heard anything at all.

"Hello," he called again. "My name is Freddie. What's yours?"

Again there was no response. Feeling very curious, Freddie rested his chin on the top of the fence and stared at his neighbor inquisitively. A few minutes passed as he waited for the horse to move, but it did not.

"Guess it must not like me," he reasoned to himself as he continued along on his jog.

For a better part of the morning, Freddie kept an eye on the motionless animal. It seemed strange to him that it could remain so perfectly still for such a long time, and not even make an attempt to walk around its paddock the way other horses did.

As the morning wore on into the afternoon, Freddie was just about convinced that it was just a painted statue put there for decoration and not a real horse at all. However, wanting to be absolutely certain of this, he stuck his head as far over the fence as he could and called to it again.

"Hello over there, I'm Freddie. I'm in the paddock next to yours. I'd like to be friends!"

This time he saw it prick up its ears and listen. It angled its head slightly to one side, but still did not turn to face him or speak a reply.

Later that day, when the farmhand came to take the horse into the barn for the night, Freddie was surprised by the way it waited so trustingly for the man to come over to it. Once on the end of the lead rope, it made no effort to look anywhere but straight ahead as it walked. Even the small terrier that barked and dashed in and out of its legs seemed to have little affect on the horse.

Freddie spent most of the rest of the night pondering the reasons why the horse had not acknowledged him. He thought that maybe he had beaten it in a race, and the horse still held a grudge against him for it. Then he considered that perhaps the horse was from South America or France and did not speak the same language he spoke.

"Hey, Thunderball, did you see that new grey horse in the paddock next to mine?" Freddie asked through the bars of his stall.

"Yes, I saw it," Thunderball answered from the stall across the way.

"Do you know who it is?"

Thunderball shook his head. "No, why?"

Freddie shrugged. "I was just wondering, that's all."

Lowering himself, Thunderball nestled into the straw for the night. He groaned loudly, then sighed as he closed his drowsy eyes. "Why don't you get some sleep, and ask it for yourself in the morning."

Freddie nodded, but he did not bother to tell him that he had already tried without having much success. Lying down, he tossed and turned and found it very hard to sleep. Having retired from racing so recently, he was used to more rigorous exercise than just being turned out in a paddock all day. He wished he was still in training so he could go to sleep with another race to look forward to, but he knew that that part of his life was over and the only races he would run in would be in his memories.

The brightness of the new day caused Freddie to squint when he walked outside the next morning. Although the winter sun was not as bright as it was the rest of the year, its rays reflected off the snow, creating the illusion that it was more radiant than it actually was.

Hearing the gate latch behind him, the thoroughbred immediately started for the far side of the paddock to see if the grey horse was already there. He found it standing in a different place than the day before. The sun's rays highlighted the dapples along its hindquarters and around its neck, and Freddie noticed that it had a jet black mane and tail with darker grey half-stockings on all four of its legs. He watched quizzically as it pawed through the snow to graze, and he could not help but wonder why it did not know that the frozen grass would be bitter until spring.

"That isn't very good to eat," he called out. "The grass tastes foul after it snows."

The horse momentarily stopped its digging and swished its tail. Bobbing its head up, it turned toward his direction, but just when Freddie thought it was going to say something, it resumed its digging again.

"Stupid horse," Freddie muttered. He felt instantly irritated that his advice had been so blatantly disregarded; but more than that, he had never seen a horse be so rude as to ignore him altogether. With an agitated snort, he started to walk away; then he reconsidered and turned back around.

"I just wanted to be friends," he said, offended. "I thought that if you were going to be there all the time, we could keep each other company, that's all."

"Who are you talking to, Freddie?" Patches asked, jumping onto the fence. She shivered a little as she sat down on the icy fencepost, and her tricolored fur stood slightly on end from the cold.

"That horse over there," he replied, pointing with his nose. "But I might as well be talking to a fencepost or a tree. It ignores everything I say and just stands in the same place all day long."

Patches looked over her shoulder at the horse, then back at Freddie.

"Well, Freddie, this isn't the racetrack," she told him. "Not everyone here knows who you are."

Freddie puffed out his chest, and gave Patches a prideful look. "What's that supposed to mean?"

Patches brushed a fleck of snow from her coat and looked at him with raised brows. "Don't you think that maybe you are acting spoiled? I think you've gotten used to everyone being impressed with you because you were a great racehorse, and you expect them to want to be your friend because of it."

"I won a lot of races and that's why everyone at the track knew me," he answered. "And I did have a lot of friends there. Just because I'm retired now doesn't mean that has to change. I'm proud of my accomplishments, and even if they don't matter as much as they used to, they're still important to me."

Patches gave him a little frown, then raised her front paw to her mouth and licked the snow off before responding. "You needn't be so touchy about it. Everyone still remembers how great you were, but you've been away from the farm a long time, and you're not as familiar here as you were at the track. This is a completely different life than what you're used to. Here it doesn't matter how many races you've won, it's how well you do as a sire. Trophies and titles are wonderful, but what matters from now on is that your children do as well as you did. Why, look at Royal Exile. Because you were such a good runner, he's got a barn all to himself—and he deserves it."

Freddie lowered his head as he considered the cat's advice, and he knew he should not be so impatient with his friend. "Maybe you're right, but I don't have any foals yet. Just because of that, I shouldn't be ignored by anyone. I was being very nice to that horse, too."

Patches offered a sympathetic smile. "It's hard for you to be in retirement, isn't it, Freddie?"

Freddie looked off into the distance. "Yes, it is a little hard, I guess. I miss the excitement of the track and the competition. I used to travel all over the country, and I looked forward to a change of scenery every now and then. Now, I'll be here forever. Don't get me wrong, this is a great place. It's just very quiet, that's all. It's very easy to get used to hearing people cheer when your name is called over the loud speaker, or having them come out in the early mornings just to watch you work. It's every horse's dream, and it's over before you know it. I loved racing, and I loved the fact that people loved to watch me run. I suppose I just feel a little lonely, that's all."

He turned away from her and walked slowly over to the part of the fence that faced Royal Exile's barn. His muscular shoulders sagged a little, and his steps were far too slow. As he stood pensively gazing upon his father's castle, what worried Freddie the most was that despite all the times he had finished first, he would be forgotten if he did not have an offspring as good as he.

Patches jumped down from the fence, scurried over to him, and rubbed against his forelegs, causing him to smile at her show of affection.

"Don't feel so bad," she comforted. "You're still my friend, and I've never even seen you race at all."

CHAPTER TWO

Freddie and Patches Solve The Mystery

NEARLY A WEEK WENT BY before Freddie attempted to make friends with the grey horse again. The holiday festivities ended with the celebration of the New Year, and as was the custom with all thoroughbreds, Freddie turned another year older on January first.

He was six and was now considered fully mature for a horse. He knew that this would be a special year because not only was he was entering a new phase in his life, but Thunderball's first crop of horses would be of racing age. While it gave Freddie a certain feeling of happiness for his friend, it also made him feel very old. Thunderball's offspring were now probably looking forward to their first race with the same anticipation that he and Freddie had when they were that age.

Their first outing together was still a vivid memory in Freddie's mind. He remembered the excitement of being in the post parade and the rush of energy he felt as he bolted from the starting gate believing that he would win even if he defied his jockey's instructions. The years and the victories that followed healed the humiliation of the defeat he suffered on that day, and now he enjoyed reminiscing about the event with Thunderball. The two retired thoroughbreds spent many long evenings fondly recalling their racing days, and Freddie was able to share the experiences that Thunderball had not been there to see. Also, because the training track was within sight of the stallion turnouts, they were able to exchange opinions on which of Thunderball's offspring looked the most talented.

Of course, Freddie's owners made a point of visiting the farm regularly. They would sometimes remark that the old nag, Mardi Gras, would probably not recognize him because he was so grown up. Freddie still cherished memories of the quarterhorse mare and how kind she had been to him when he was a foal.

Other people came to the farm to see him as well. They were usually people who had followed his racing career and came to pay their respects. However, as the weeks passed, there were fewer and fewer of them until the visits from his owners were the only thing he could count on.

"Don't worry about it, Fred," Thunderball told him. "It was like that with all of us. They treat you special at the start, but come spring, there'll be another Derby horse to watch, and you'll just be part of racing history. That's the way it should be. You have to let someone else enjoy the spotlight the way you did."

"But I won the Kentucky Derby," Freddie remarked, feeling suddenly lonely for the affection of his fans.

"So did your father," Thunderball replied, "and that will never change. Forever and ever your name plate will be up in the clubhouse, and when it's Derby week, there will still be people who come to see you and tell you how great you were. But that's only one week out of the year. The rest of the time you're just one of us."

Freddie nodded, and a nostalgic cast showed in his eyes. "Well, at least I have that."

"Oh, you'll have plenty more too. It's really fun to see the young horses playing in the pasture the way we did and dreaming of becoming great racehorses. I think I'm looking forward to my offspring going to the track more than I looked forward to it myself. Just wait, once you lay your eyes on one of your own foals, you'll truly understand how wonderful they are."

Freddie tried to find comfort in his friend's wisdom. He was sure that when his youngsters were ready to run that he would treat them with the same exuberance as Thunderball. But until his first crop was foaled, the only thing he looked forward to was his daily ride by an exercise rider to keep him physically fit. He enjoyed the late morning jogs, and when it was raining or snowing outside, he was exercised on a treadmill in the training barn. At first, he thought it was an odd contraption because a conveyor belt would move beneath his feet to make him run in place. He was just as tired when he was finished there as when he galloped outside, but it was always a bit disillusioning to work so hard to go nowhere.

Still, with all the comings and goings of visitors and horses in training, the one thing that intrigued Freddie the most was in the paddock beside his. The grey thoroughbred who kept its back turned had become the great mystery. Even Patches started to wonder why any horse would behave so strangely. If it were not for the Jack Russell terrier who protected it, she would have gone to investigate for herself. One night, when Freddie, Thunderball, and Patches were all talking in the barn after the lights were out, the question of the horse's identity found its way into their conversation.

"Hey, Fred, what about that grey? Has it said anything to you yet?" Thunderball asked.

Freddie shook his head no.

"Why do you think that is?"

Freddie shrugged. "I don't think it has anything against me personally. It just doesn't seem to want to talk to anyone, and it just stands in the same place all day long. I thought maybe it had leg problems, but it walks just fine when it's being led by a groom."

"I can't figure it out either," Patches added. "In all the years I've lived here, I've never seen a horse who didn't want to run at least some of the time."

"Maybe it's just shy," Thunderball said kindly.

"Maybe," Freddie responded. "I think it must be lonely with only that little dog for company. I'd really like to be its friend."

"Patches, I know that the dog is a hazard for you, but maybe you could get close enough to tell it that Freddie wants to be friends," Thunderball suggested.

Patches' hair stood on end. "Not a chance. Jack Russell terriers are bred for hunting foxes, and they've been known to kill. If I got more than a few feet into that paddock, I'm afraid it would get me. I remember when it first moved here, I was sleeping on top of the hay bales and it leaped up on them and nearly bit my tail! I ran as fast as I could to get away from it, but it chased me all the way to the tree in front of the main house, and then parked itself at the base of it until well after dark. I really think I used up one of my nine lives that day."

Both Thunderball and Freddie tried to hide their smirks. They knew she was being serious, but her story and her seriousness seemed somewhat comical to them.

"It isn't funny," she said impatiently. "I was really scared— more scared than I was the time the coyote chased me when I was a kitten."

"We're sorry," Freddie said with a good-natured chuckle. "It's just that I'm so curious about that horse, and you're the only one who can get close enough to it to say anything. I know it's a lot to ask, but if you could just try, I'd really appreciate it. Surely, I don't want anything to happen to you. If that terrier comes after you, you should head straight back to me. I'll handle him."

Patches gave him an uncertain look. "I don't know. That little dog is so fast that I'm afraid he'd have me for dinner before I could even make it to you."

"It would be worth at least one try," Thunderball persuaded. "Just think of the good you'd be doing for the horse and for Freddie. After all, you only used up one life the last time you were chased. You still have eight lives left."

The calico cat shook her head. "Not a chance. I know you two are my best friends, but I can't help you this time and that's final."

It was early the next morning when Patches started out across the snowy ground to reach the grey thoroughbred. Using all her stealth, she crept so low to the ground that the ice stung her belly and sent shivers through her body. Her eyes were wide with uncertainty, and at the slightest sound or movement, she would stop in her tracks and look around to be sure it was not the terrier. The thud of her racing heart sounded so loud inside her head that she was sure it could easily be heard by the dog wherever he might be on the farm. Her tiny cat paws left shallow imprints in the snow, and her tail waggled with each step she took.

Keeping her eyes fixed on the mysterious horse, she moved steadily and quietly nearer as both Freddie and Thunderball looked on from their paddocks. When she was almost to it, she stopped and took one last look over her shoulder at her two equine friends, fearing that if the terrier was waiting, it could be the last time she would ever see them. As she did this, she realized just how far out of familiar territory she had ventured, and a feeling of absolute helplessness overcame her. It did not matter that Freddie and Thunderball's paddocks were on either side because at that moment, she was out in the open field with only her wits and her speed to protect her.

Drawing closer to the grey, she noticed that it had one ear cocked in her direction. Placing one paw in front of the other, Patches came still closer. The horse pointed its nose her way and sniffed the air to catch a scent. The cat lowered her gaze and kept her eyes fixed in front of her. She wanted to rely on her hearing not her sight, because she knew that if the dog was coming to get her, she would hear him long before she saw him.

By the time she was at the horse's foreleg, the fur on her belly was soaking wet, and the pads of her feet were numb from the snow. Slowly raising her eyes, she looked up at the grey thoroughbred and could not believe what she saw. It sent such a shock through her that before she could speak a word of greeting to it, she instinctively let out a horrific screech — a screech so loud that it was like a siren sounding to the very enemy she had been trying to avoid.

"Patches run!" she heard Freddie suddenly shout.

"Run, Patches, run!" Thunderball's frantic voice echoed in her ringing ears.

All at once, she felt a set of teeth sink into her tail followed by a menacing growl from the terrier as she was yanked backward. Reaching around with one paw, she swiped her claw across his face slicing the tip of his nose.

The dog released her, and despite her efforts to run from it, it was back on her in an instant. The grey horse started pacing fretfully from side to side, and once one of its hooves almost landed directly on Patches, but she scrambled out of its way.

Freddie and Thunderball were both running wildly along the pasture fence, neighing loudly as the terrier clenched his teeth on the nape of Patches' neck and started shaking her. Amidst the confusion and pain, the cat caught a glimpse of Freddie standing up on his back legs and snorting his command for the terrier to release her.

"Help me! Help me!" she screeched, her shrill voice filled with fear. "Freddie, Thunderball, do something. He's going to kill me!"

There was so much commotion that she was not sure what happened next. She saw Freddie in mid-air, then there were not just four legs shuffling around her, there were eight.

"Let her alone!" she heard Freddie demand as one of his big hooves came crashing down just inches away from the dog.

"No!" the terrier retorted, in a growl that sounded more like it came from the idling engine of the feed truck than from a dog. "My job is to protect this horse."

"And mine is to protect Patches, so you'd better let her go," Freddie argued. He bent his muscular neck, and took the dog's ear between his lips, pulling it as hard as he could. The terrier yelped and released the cat. Then Freddie felt a sharp nip on the end of his nose, but he kept a firm hold on him until Patches could limp to safety.

When he was sure she was all right, he let go of the snarling dog and the angry little terrier started nipping at his heels.

"Don't think you can scare me, you thousand-pound bully!" he yelled angrily. "I've got a job to do!"

Lifting his legs in a quick jig, Freddie looked like a dancing carousel horse as he tried to avoid being bitten. Then losing his patience altogether, he lunged at the dog, but it started running circles around him.

"What's the matter, can't you take it?" it taunted. "You think you can push your way into this pasture and not have me to contend with."

Freddie looked at him sharply. "I wasn't trying to hurt anybody and neither was Patches. We only wanted to ask this horse to be our friend. We meant no harm," he explained.

At that moment he suddenly remembered that through all the confusion, the grey had not made a noise, nor had it tried to run away. Turning to it, Freddie was about to apologize for what had just happened when he saw what had caused Patches' shocked reaction.

The horse appeared perfectly normal except that in the place where its eyes should have been, it had only sockets. From the way they were covered with smooth grey fur, it was plain that it had been born that way. Now Freddie completely understood why it did not run like other horses and seemed afraid to talk with strangers. It was totally blind.

Taking a deep breath, he looked apologetically down at the ferocious terrier and understood why he was so protective.

"Hey, somebody get a lead rope," the voice of a farmhand was heard. "The new stallion has jumped the fence!"

There was the scuffle of feet and before Freddie knew it, two farmhands were leading him out of the pasture. The terrier followed them all the way to the barn, nipping at his long red tail as he was taken to his stall, and the barred door slammed shut behind him.

CHAPTER THREE

Woodrow Tells All

"YOU DESERVE TO BE LOCKED UP for what you did!" the terrier declared as he marched like a toy soldier back and forth in front of Freddie's stall.

With one brow raised, the stallion stared down at him through the iron bars. He could not believe that such a small creature could be so bold. He was little more than a foot high with stout, muscular legs that looked like springs when he ran. With the exception of a black and brown marking covering one eye like a pirate's patch and a perfect black circle on the top of his head, his coat was primarily white. His fur was broken into different textures. Along his back and around his face were wiry curls, but the remainder of his thick body was perfectly smooth. His tail was only as long as a gate handle, and when it wagged, his whole body seemed to vibrate comically from the motion. His voice was gravelly and seemed too deep in tone to come from such a miniature body.

"I didn't do anything but try to save Patches," Freddie stated in his defense. "You're the one that should be put behind bars for grabbing her by the neck like that. And one

29

other thing, I'm not locked up, I live in this stall. See the nameplate on the door—that's me."

The terrier squinted his dark button eyes as he read the engraved brass plate. "Rue Royale, by Royal Exile out of Romantic Myth," he said aloud, then sat back on his haunches and soberly shook his head. "Sure, I know all about you. The farmhands said you won the Kentucky Derby and were voted Horse of the Year. They call you Freddie, but I'll tell you what, Freddie, by the look of your pedigree, I'd have thought you'd behave better than the way you did this morning."

Freddie stomped his foot down hard in frustration. "I wasn't trying to hurt the grey, I was just trying to save Patches, and I really think you overreacted! After all, what can a cat do to hurt a horse? You didn't have to be so rough on her."

The dog cocked his head to one side, then resumed his pacing as he considered Freddie's explanation. "You know, I really don't have anything against cats, I suppose I'm just very protective when it comes to Rosie. She—"

"Rosie?" Freddie interrupted. "Is that her name?"

"Yes, and as I was saying—"

"Is she going to live here permanently?" Freddie broke in again.

The dog heaved a sigh. "Will you let me finish?" he demanded.

Realizing what poor manners he was showing, Freddie shrank back in embarrassment. "Sorry," he mumbled.

"That's all right," the terrier went on with a nod. "But as I was saying, ever since the day she was born I've been with her. She has no eyes, never has had them and never will. So she relies on me to look out for her."

A feeling of sympathy came over Freddie as he thought about the grey mare. He could not imagine what it would be like never to see another horse, or a bird sweeping across the sky, or to watch lightning strike on a stormy night.

"Is that why she is so timid?" he asked.

"She's not timid; she's cautious. There's a whole world of things out there that she knows nothing about," the dog answered. "For instance, when you run you can see everything in front of you, so you know just how fast to go, and when to slow down, right?"

"Well sure, if I didn't know when to slow down, I could run into a fence or tree and really hurt myself."

"Exactly. But Rosie can't do that. The first week after she was born, she got spooked and tried to run away. She hit the corner of the stall door and split her face open. It's just a good thing that she had a nice owner who cared about her because anyone else would have put her down. Most folks would think a blind horse is good for nothing."

He stopped pacing and his thoughts seemed to drift for a moment. His mischievous dark eyes lost their sparkle and Freddie could tell that he was remembering something very sad.

"But that isn't true," he continued after a moment. "Rosie is special. In all my life I've never met anyone as kind and understanding as she is. She and I take care of each other. We're best friends."

Freddie bowed his head. "I would like to be her friend too. I was just retired from racing and, well, to tell you the truth, the days can get pretty long when you spend them in a paddock all alone. The only time I have someone to visit with besides Patches is at night when Thunderball is brought in."

The dog's brow furrowed and he eyed Freddie doubtfully.

"Why are you looking at me like that?" Freddie asked.

"I didn't expect you to say something like that," he responded. He moved closer to the stall door, and Freddie could see the stub of his tail start to wag. "I thought all you race stallions were too tough to have feelings like that."

"Just because I'm off the track doesn't mean I don't have a heart," Freddie replied. "To say I don't have feelings would be like me saying that just because Rosie can't see, she doesn't know what life is about. None of us are perfect."

The dog made no effort to answer. He looked back at Freddie for a long moment, and the thoroughbred thought that he was mocking him. Then, the terrier started walking toward the barn door.

Freddie stared after him wondering if he had insulted him somehow and he was leaving because of it. The outside light cast a long shadow that made his compact body look as though a giant was standing in the shedrow.

"Are you just going to leave without even saying good-bye?" Freddie called.

At that the dog stopped, and with his tail still wagging, he turned to him with a sincere smile.

"Tell your cat friend that I'm sorry about this morning," he said. "Tell her that I misunderstood her intentions and it won't happen again."

"I will," Freddie answered. "And maybe you could explain things to Rosie as well."

"I will," he answered. With bold, deliberate steps he disappeared around the corner of the barn, then came back and poked his head through the doorway. "Hey, Fred? It's all right if I call you Fred, isn't it?"

"Yes."

"Good. From now on, you can call me Woodrow."

Freddie smiled back at him. "Thanks, Woodrow."

"Thanks, Fred."

That night a snow storm blew in that kept Freddie in his stall for the next two days. The fallen snow created a stark white plain of the farm that was only interrupted by the occasional sight of a fox zigzagging through the ice in search of game. The steady hoot of an owl in a nearby tree sounded like a clock ticking away the dark hours, and even the normally industrious squirrels were scared into their burrows by the severe cold.

The weather eased on the third day, and Patches returned with a her tail wrapped in gauze and the fur on her neck shaved where Woodrow's teeth had punctured the skin. She meowed a very distressing story of having to spend the night at the vet's office.

"Well, were they nice to you there?" Freddie asked, worried that she had been mistreated.

"Oh, sure, they were really, really nice to me," she answered, curling her bandaged tail around in front of her. "I just didn't like the shots they gave me. They said it was to fight off infection. I even had to have stitches. Those didn't hurt too much because one shot numbed my entire tail." She wrinkled her nose in displeasure and Freddie chuckled at her funny expression.

"Thank you for trying, Patches, and I'm really sorry that I talked you into going over there," Freddie apologized. "I didn't think this would happen."

Patches touched a paw to her bandage and shrugged. "I know you didn't think I'd get hurt. I really just wanted to do it for you because you are my friend. Besides, I don't think this would have happened at all if I hadn't screeched so loud when I saw the grey's face. I feel like I ought to apologize to her. She must feel very self-conscious to begin with, not to mention the way that I reacted. It just was not what I expected. It must have hurt her feelings. I know it would've hurt mine."

Freddie smiled a reply and gazed thoughtfully out the window. The fluffy snowflakes were dropping from the sky like falling stars as they changed the whole world into a silent, sparkling white. He remembered that when he was a foal, he would watch as the snowflakes landed on his mother's coat. For a brief instant, he would be fascinated by their beautiful designs until the heat of her body caused them to melt.

"I wonder how you would explain snow to her?" he asked.

Patches rose from her place, and slipping between the bars of his stall, she jumped up on the window ledge and looked out.

"I can't imagine," she answered. She looked deep into Freddie's eyes, enchanted by their rich brown color and the jet black pupil at their center. She thought about the grey mare, and could not help but feel a deep regret that she would never be able to look into Freddie's eyes and see how kind they were. Then, the calico lightly touched her paw to the bridge of his long nose just as Freddie rested his chin on the sill. He had a wistful look about him as he let out a heavy sigh.

"You really like her don't you, Freddie?" Patches asked.

Freddie blinked slowly as his expression became one of tender yearning. "I don't know if you can really like someone by seeing them only once," he answered sincerely. "I've never even met Rosie, but I can honestly tell you that I don't pity her because she is blind. Instead, I admire her for having the courage to live without sight."

Neither the horse nor the cat said anything more, and resting their heads together, they watched the frosty crystals spread across the empty pastures as though someone was shining a filtered light on them from above.

CHAPTER FOUR

The Introduction

THE SKY REMAINED a dismal grey, and the snow continued to fall in endless sprinkles until the trees drooped from the icy ridges that formed along their branches. Although he enjoyed the cozy warmth of the barn, Freddie was quite anxious for the storm to pass so he could get out and run again. The stablehands took turns walking the stallions around the shed-row to stretch their legs, and they also worked them on the treadmill, but it could not replace that feeling of galloping freely in the fresh air and wide open fields.

Days later, when the sun finally did fight its way out of the clouds, Freddie awoke to the sound of dripping water outside his window. Looking up, he realized that it was coming from an icicle that had begun to melt. Then seeing that the sky radiated a golden light, he knew that his freedom was about to be restored.

Rising sleepily, he shook his body loose of the straw, whinnied loudly, then shook himself again.

"What's all the noise about?" Thunderball asked, sleepily raising his head and looking around with blurry eyes.

"The sun is out!" Freddie replied jubilantly.

Slowly getting to his feet, Thunderball took an uneven step forward. The leg that had been hurt racing had now become arthritic, and the damp weather always made it quite stiff.

"Good," he said. "At least we'll be able to leave the barn, and you might even get to meet the grey mare."

Freddie looked at him out of the corner of his eye, but did not answer. The truth was that he was very excited to be introduced to Rosie—excited and nervous as well. When he received his morning flake of hay, he gobbled it down as fast as he could just so he might go out earlier. However, to his dismay, it was noon before his handler came for him.

Striding past the long rows of stalls, he gazed into the distant pasture and saw that the grey mare was already out. He had no idea as to what he would say to her first. All he knew was that when he saw her familiar outline against the white ground, the loneliness that had so disturbed him while he was penned up during the storm seemed to disappear.

He waited as patiently as he could for the shank to be unclasped from his halter. Once he mistakenly thought he was loose and he jerked his head hard to the side, accidently pulling his handler off balance.

"Just take it easy, fella. I know how good it feels to be out again," he said understandingly as he patted Freddie on the forehead.

A moment later, Freddie was running along the fence, squealing with delight. The cold morning air formed clouds in front of his glazed red nostrils as he exhaled, and his flesh tingled as he kicked his legs out behind him. His tail was sticking straight up, causing the strands to appear like a cascading chestnut shower in the breeze. Lifting his knees in a playful gait, he trotted to all four corners of his paddock and whinnied his delight to the frozen world.

The winter white plain in front of him donned tracks of rabbits and foxes that ranged over a hilltop and off into the woods. There was a red squirrel in a nearby tree munching on some dried corn that he had stolen from the grain bin. Skillfully shifting his weight to only three legs, Freddie stretched out one foreleg and rubbed his brow against his knee. Then he straightened up and walked over to watch a family of partridges as they exited the wood pile alongside the barn. They bustled off into the shrubbery, and the snow that had clumped on the leaves fell down around them as their plump bodies nudged each other along.

Turning to face Rosie's paddock, Freddie felt a surge of excitement as he saw Woodrow leading her over to meet him. The terrier's legs were so short and the snow was so deep that every step was actually a leap forward. From where Freddie was standing, it appeared as though he were simply bobbing up and down and not making much progress at all.

Freddie laughed to himself at the sight of it and wondered what life would be like if he always had to look up at everyone. As it was, he was a very tall horse, and other than birds in trees, he seldom found himself having to look up at any other animal. Then he considered Rosie's loss of sight, and he realized how much he had taken his own vision for granted. He had no idea what it would be like to live in total darkness every day of his life. Looking at her now as she approached, he was taken by her prideful gait. Whether it was her absolute trust of Woodrow or her own self-confidence showing through, each step she took was a stately one.

As the sun highlighted her lovely dapple coat, Freddie saw that her conformation was that of a dazzling, vigorous thoroughbred. Her ebony mane blew in the crisp breeze and she had a perfect white blaze down her nose. It seemed only a moment had gone by before she stopped directly in front of him, as Woodrow hopped over the lowest fence board and came alongside Freddie's front leg.

"Fred," he said politely, "this is Rosie."

From the way his eyes glittered when he said her name, it was clear that he possessed a deep admiration for the mare; and from the manner in which she cocked her ears to follow him, it was also obvious that she was distinctly aware of his every move.

"It's nice to meet—" Freddie started to speak, but was interrupted by Woodrow.

"Just hold on a minute," he said curtly. "I'm not finished yet."

He hopped back over the fence, and taking a place beside Rosie, he sat up on his haunches and gave a small, excitable bark. "Rosie, I'd like you to meet my friend Fred."

Looking over at the stallion he gave him a nod. "All right you can say whatever you were going to say now."

Freddie bowed his sleek neck and jabbed the earth with one hoof in a gallant gesture of greeting. He felt as though he were being indulged by someone very important. Rosie blew a tiny snort, then cautiously sniffed the air in front of her.

The chestnut stallion watched her silently, finding that he was completely used to the sight of her, and the smooth grey fur that covered her hollow eye sockets did not seem strange at all. What did seem almost unbearable for him to suppose was the loneliness that this mare must have endured all these years with only a single dog to attend her. He felt disturbed by it, not as though it would harm him in any way, but that for all the wonderful memories he had from his days as a foal through the glory of the racetrack, they would mean nothing to her. She had lived in a world of smell and touch, and the noises that she heard from the sound of an owl hooting in a tree at night, to the chugging of the feed truck coming down the lane, held no image for her at all.

"Hello, Fred," she said in a sweet, but cautious voice.

Freddie cleared his throat and puffed out his chest. "Hello, Rosie," he stammered. Then he turned away because he was afraid she would be able to tell how bashful he suddenly felt, because for all of his strength and boldness, it came to him all too clearly that this humble mare had shown more bravery in facing life than he ever had during his entire racing career.

"Is something wrong?" she asked, sensing that he had turned his back to her.

Freddie whirled back around and dipped his head, then looked up at her uncertainly. "No, nothing at all," he answered, trying to sound more carefree than he really was.

An unpretentious smile pursed her lips and she sighed. "It's all right," she told him. "I'm used to others thinking I look ugly. It doesn't bother me though, because I'll never be able to see how ugly they think I am."

"Oh, I don't think you're ugly!" he protested. "I just don't know what to say, that's all." He found himself smiling back at her as he moved closer and stuck his head over the top of the fence. There was a tense moment when neither horse knew what to say next, then Rosie broke the silence.

"Woodrow told me that you have only been at this farm for a short while," she said. "This is my first time here. Before this, I was at a farm in Florida. It never snowed there. It's hard for me to get used to it because all of the scents of the flowers and the trees disappear, and it makes everything so quiet that I can hardly tell when someone is coming. I didn't even hear your friend Patches until she was right beside me, and I didn't know what happened until Woodrow told me about it later. I hope she will be all right."

"Patches will be fine," Freddie assured her. "Did you like living in Florida?"

The mare hesitated a moment and as her head drooped down a little, her smile faded. "Yes, my owner was a veterinarian, and he used to take very good care of me. They said that when I was born, no one but he thought I'd survive. He and Woodrow have helped me learn how to get by without being able to see."

"Did your owner move out here too?" Freddie asked.

Rosie shook her head. "No, something happened to him. I don't like to think about it because I'd rather remember how he used to feed me apples and molasses. He was a very kind man."

Freddie looked over at Woodrow and raised his brows questioningly. The terrier met his eye, then gave a sorrowful shake of his head as if to signal that it was too sad a memory for her to continue talking about it.

"I like to remember Florida too. It was always very warm there," Rosie continued.

"Well, this isn't Florida, that's for sure, but it's a wonderful place," Freddie responded, trying to lift her spirits. "It's a little quiet for me, especially after living at the racetrack, but I was raised here, so I guess it'll seem like home before I know it. I have got a lot of good friends here, like Thunderball. He and I were foals together, we went all the way through breaking and training with each other, and we even raced in the same maiden race! My mother, Romantic Myth, lives over in the broodmare pasture, and my sire, Royal Exile, has his own special barn. It's right over there."

Freddie started to motion with his nose in the direction of Royal Exile's private stud barn, then suddenly remembered that to Rosie it would not make the slightest bit of difference.

"Is it beautiful?" she asked.

"Yes, Rosie, it is," he answered, touched by her sincere interest.

"Can you describe it to me?"

Freddie took in a gulp of air and not knowing why, his eyes started to tear. He looked over at Royal Exile's barn, then back at Rosie. "I'll try. It's made of white clapboard with a green steeple on the top that is lit up at night. There are sliding doors of varnished wood at the front and the back of it, and all the windows have painted green shutters."

"How many windows are there?" she asked. From the tone of her voice he could tell that she was amused by his efforts.

"Two on each of the four walls," Freddie went on proudly. "They built him his own barn because he has sired so many winning offspring. He's even had some winners on the turf in Europe and the United Kingdom. As for me, I never raced on the turf, only on the dirt."

Rosie nodded her head. "And what is the difference between running on the dirt and running on the turf?"

"Well, here in America most of the races are run on dirt because most racecourses are in the middle of cities. They have a turf course, but there is usually only one turf race per day on a race card," he explained. "I hear that in Europe the race meet travels from town to town, so each week they are in a different place. They are all run on the grass because there is more open space to hold the races, and the grass has plenty of time to grow back. Here, most of the racing is usually at one site for few weeks, or even a few months at a time."

"I see," Rosie replied, interested. "Did you race a lot?"

Freddie nodded, but she did not respond.

"Fred, did you run in a lot of races?" she asked again.

Freddie suddenly felt foolish because he realized that she was unable to see his gestures.

"Yes," he answered. "I ran in some good races. I didn't win them all, but I'd never want to boast because I've had some victories that made me feel very proud."

Rosie bent her head to one side, and her brow furrowed as though she was not sure what he meant. Then it smoothed out again, and she smiled. "I don't think you are boasting. It's good to like yourself because if you rely on what other people think of you, it can make you very unhappy. There were a few times when I felt badly about myself because I'd overhear someone saying that I was not good for anything because I have no eyes, but in a way, I feel like it can be a kind of gift because I'm free to view things with my heart. Then, the way I feel about myself and others is always the truth."

Freddie's smile broadened. Rosie really was as special as Woodrow had said. "And what does your heart tell you about me?" he asked playfully.

"That you and I are going to be good company for each other," she answered sweetly.

She took a step closer, and as if she could see him perfectly, she rested her head on the fence rail right next to his.

CHAPTER FIVE

Bluegrass Summer

THE WEEKS THAT FOLLOWED brought a slightly warmer rain than the rain that preceded the earlier snows. The sun, which had withdrawn to a dull presence for the months between November and February, shined longer and longer each day, until its rays were strong enough to melt the frost and nurture the green sprigs of new grass. The squirrels chirped a cheerful song, and even the duck that lived in a nearby pond emerged from the duck house one morning with a string of six ducklings chattering loudly behind her as they plopped into the water for the very first time.

It was a happy time for Freddie. As soon as he was fed, groomed, and turned out, he would gallop to the far side of his paddock and wait for Rosie. She had easily learned the route to the place where he waited for her each day, and there was a well-trodden path that had not been grassed over with the arrival of spring.

For the chestnut stallion and the grey mare, the time that they were together was the best part of the day. Freddie was thoroughly enchanted with Rosie. She had such compassion

for others and was genuinely interested in what he had to share. Suddenly, he found that the many things that seemed commonplace prior to their meeting had taken on new meaning. The color of the pink blossoms on the cherry trees or the fluttering purple and green wings of a hummingbird were a challenge for him to describe.

In turn, Rosie was absolutely delighted that he made such a grand effort bring to life that which, up until now, had been concealed in a world of darkness. Yet, the one thing Freddie never spoke to her about were his racing days. It was not because he had forgotten about them, rather it was because Rosie's company made him miss them less. There was no longer any reason to reminisce about the past because what was happening each and every day made him just as glad.

One afternoon when Freddie and Rosie were grazing nose to nose with only the lower fence plank between them, the sound of galloping hooves startled Rosie. Pricking her ears forward, she listened for a moment, then snorted in alarm and moved closer in Freddie's direction. She did this with such haste that she accidently bumped into the fence, and thinking that it was something to fear, she wheeled back around and bolted in the opposite direction.

The frantic cry of a loose weanling frightened her more, and before Freddie could say anything to calm her, she was running away from him.

"Rosie wait! There's nothing to be afraid of!" he hollered to her.

The mare was deaf to his call as she made another sweeping turn barely missing the far paddock gate.

The thud of the hooves jarred Woodrow from where he had been snoozing beneath a tree. He sprang to attention just as the weanling breezed by, and assuming that the young horse had done something wrong, he ran after him.

Nipping at the heels of the gangly colt, he gave it such a scare that it kicked behind him and connected with Woodrow's muscular little body. As if he had been shot out of a cannon, the terrier was instantly propelled back in the direction he had come. When he hit the ground, he rolled, then jumped to his feet and darted after the weanling again.

"I'm going to get you for that!" he growled as he dashed across Freddie's paddock and headed off the runaway horse.

The colt stopped in his tracks as Woodrow began running around him. His bark was gruff and intimidating, and every time the horse tried to rush one way, Woodrow was there to stop him. The whites of the weanling's eyes were showing, and his hustling steps made divots in the downy soft grass.

"What do you think you're doing making a scene like this?" Woodrow demanded. "Don't you know you could get somebody hurt causing such a commotion?"

The youngster stopped, and lowering his head, sniffed the dog. Then he raised his nose in the air and squealed.

"Oh, be quiet," Woodrow scolded. "There's nothing wrong with you except that you're a big chicken."

The young horse wrinkled his nose and gave the terrier a mean look. "I'm not a chicken—I'm a horse."

"Then act like one!" Woodrow told him. "Quit all this running around like you don't know what the heck is going on. There's not a reason in the world for you to be having such a fit."

The runaway's eyes widened until it looked like they could not get any larger. "Yes, there is," he stated.

"No, there's not," Woodrow countered firmly.

"Is to," he insisted.

"Is not," Woodrow argued.

The horse stomped its foot down once, then twice. "There is too! They want to put a bit in my mouth," he said with a quiver in his voice.

Woodrow heaved an impatient sigh and sat down in front of him. He looked the weanling up and down, then shook his head in disgust. "I swear! You youngsters make things hard on yourselves. Do you think that it's going to kill you to have a bit in your mouth?"

"No, but it looks like it would hurt."

"It won't hurt if you don't fight it," the terrier responded. His tone was more wise now than angry. "The only way anyone is ever going to be able to ride you is if you learn to take the bit."

The colt looked at him suspiciously. "How would you know? You've never had to take a bit."

Woodrow rolled his eyes and got to his feet. "Take a look at the size of me. Of course, no one has ever ridden me, but if you look in any one of these pastures, all of the horses have had to go through the very same thing as you and it didn't kill them. So wise up! You know, you big guys could sure learn something from us little guys. You think you're so tough that you can conquer the obstacles of life with brute force. Those of us that aren't as strong have to adjust to life. We can't fight it. I learned a long time ago that things roll along at their own pace, so you might as well enjoy them. Like taking the bit, for instance. If you just relax into it, you'll find you'll have a lot more fun. Your only other choice is to become a rogue, then everyone will hate you because you hate yourself."

The horse tilted its head to one side questioningly, and just as he opened his mouth to reply, an exercise rider came alongside him. Snapping a lead rope onto his halter, he patted him on the neck while talking to him calmly.

"You're all right," he soothed. "Nobody is going to hurt you."

The colt responded by following his lead, and when they were almost at the track Woodrow heard the rider and trainer laugh. "Well, at least we know this one can run," the trainer said.

"I guess so," the exercise rider replied, then turned and looked back at Woodrow. "Thanks for helping us catch him, buddy."

Woodrow barked a response, then started back to see if Rosie was all right. When he got to her paddock he found her standing with Freddie protectively looking over her. The stallion had his neck craned over the fence and was nuzzling her mane. Even at a distance, Woodrow could see that she was still trembling, and while he knew there was nothing he could have done to prevent the weanling from getting loose, he still felt somewhat guilty for being asleep when it happened instead of at Rosie's side.

"You know she acts brave, but when something as simple as this happens I really see how fragile she is," Freddie whispered to the terrier.

Woodrow nodded, then turned his attention to Rosie. "You all right, gal?" he asked, trying not to sound worried. He knew that she felt embarrassed so rather than make her feel wrong for it, he wanted to treat it as though it was nothing out of the ordinary.

"Sure," she said in a small voice. "I shouldn't have been so frightened, I guess. I just heard the whinnying and the running and thought that something horrible had happened."

Freddie looked at her remorsefully. At that moment he realized how unfair it was that a horse that was so sensitive ever had to fear anything.

"Rosie," he said in a voice so gentle that only she could hear him. "You never have to apologize to me, I'm your friend. You had no way of knowing whether that horse was going to harm you, or if he was running from something else that could have hurt you, so you don't need to make any excuses. But I will promise you one thing. From this minute on, if you trust me, I'll never let anything happen to you. When you don't know what's taking place or if you feel afraid, just tell me, and I'll take care of us both. All right?"

Freddie could see the mare's tense muscles relax as her lips quivered into a tender smile. She lowered her ears and pressed the side of her face against his. She said nothing for a moment, then answered him with a tiny kiss just below one ear.

"Yes, Fred," she replied. "I know I can be sure of you."

By the middle of the summer, the tops of the long grass had sprouted, and the hills of central Kentucky took on the lush blue tint for which the state was known. The air was humid and warm, and thunderstorms were a predictable occurrence.

Freddie loved the feel of the summer rain on his back, and even though Rosie was wary of the booming thunder and crack of the lightning, she soon came to enjoy the brief showers as a release from the summer heat. When the sun was out, she and Freddie would stand at the fence with their necks wrapped around each other and doze, and true to his promise,

she always felt safe whenever he was nearby. Even Patches
and Woodrow had come to tolerate each other. Woodrow had
apologized to Patches for biting her tail, but in turn he made
her apologize for sneaking up on him. The calico found it a
little enough gesture to bring about peace.

On very hot nights, the horses were sometimes allowed to
stay outside, all except Royal Exile. Over the past few years,
his runners had been doing so well that he was now worth
more than the rest of the stallions on the farm put together.
Of course no thoroughbred was ever treated with less care
than any other, but there was something considerably different about the way Royal Exile was handled.

Because he had his own barn and turn out, Freddie seldom
had a chance to speak with him except when they occasionally passed each other as they were being led from their afternoon baths or to the veterinarian's office for regular
examinations. The regal stud would meet Freddie's eye, and
offer his son a distinguished nod. Freddie would proudly nod
back, and father and son would have a hurried, but pleasant
exchange. There was never any doubt in Freddie's mind that
Royal Exile cared for him deeply.

However, for all the wisdom and genuine care that Royal
Exile showed to the horses and animals around him, there
was only one human that he had ever trusted, and that was
his groom. This young man, who had worked around horses
all of his life, began caring for Royal Exile when the thoroughbred first appeared on the track as a very talented two-
year-old. From the moment man and horse laid eyes on each
other, both knew that they were destined to be lifelong partners. As Royal Exile proved himself a great champion, his
groom often said that a horse like him only came around once

in a lifetime. When Royal Exile assumed a career as a stallion, his groom moved to the farm with him.

The stallion had mentioned to Freddie that the reason he did not like most people was because their voices were much too loud when they spoke to him, and they touched him far too roughly. He had also told Freddie that he sometimes found them foolish in the way they were so intolerant with each other and often gave less than their best effort in life.

"A champion racehorse would never do anything like that," he had said. "Only fools live a halfhearted life."

So each day at about four-thirty, Royal Exile's groom would come to take him back to the barn. Rain or shine, he was always there. At the sight of him, the stallion, who never acknowledged anyone else, would stroll to the gate and follow him wherever he needed to go. The only day this did not happen was when the groom's first baby was born.

On that afternoon, the curious eyes of six young stallions watched as another groom headed out to Royal Exile's paddock to catch him. What made this seem so unusual was that none of the stallions recognized the young man who bobbed his head as he walked and looked about with careless eyes. A lead rope dangled loosely in one hand, and in the other hand he held a cigarette. When he unlatched the stallion's paddock gate, he dropped the half-smoked stub before beginning the troublesome task ahead.

From the start, it was obvious that Royal Exile did not appreciate the presence of a stranger in his paddock. He flared his nostrils and puffed out his chest as he let loose of a series of threatening snorts and whinnies which, in horse language, meant he would rather the intruder leave him alone altogether.

This display annoyed the handler who, without even the slightest gesture of greeting or respect, walked directly up to the horse. When he was almost within reach, Royal Exile's tail stuck straight up in the air like flag signaling his displeasure. The muscles in his shoulders bulged, and in an instant, he was circling his pasture at a crisp trot.

"Whoa, whoa, you just settle down now," the handler impatiently demanded. Royal Exile halted, then started to jog a tight circle around him, neighing all the while in an anxious tone.

"Settle down now!" the man commanded, and the anger in his voice triggered the stallion. With the next stride, Royal Exile was bolting across the grass with such speed that it appeared as though he would run right through the fence. But with perfect agility, he stopped just in front of it, turned, and charged back at the man.

At first, it looked as though the handler would stand his ground, but at the very last minute his nerve deserted him, and he scuffled out of the way of the oncoming horse.

Freddie looked over at Thunderball with raised brows. "Do you think my father was planning to stop?" he asked uncertainly.

Thunderball shrugged. "I don't know, Royal Exile would never deliberately harm anyone. Maybe he just thinks this guy is being rude, I mean he could have at least said hello before trying to grab him like that. He would have done it if he were meeting a person for the first time, so why should a horse be any different? Your father is used to being treated with respect, and I think he was just trying to show him who's boss."

Both of the young thoroughbreds watched as, apparently satisfied that he had asserted his dominance, the stallion let the man approach. He stood facing him as the handler grabbed him roughly by the halter. It was clear to all who knew Royal Exile that he was only tolerating such treatment because he did not truly want to hurt anyone. Then, the groom jerked hard on the chain, and the stallion's natural response was to yank his head away. When he did, the man hit him hard on the neck with the leather strap.

"Stupid horse," he grunted, and Royal Exile's eyes narrowed angrily.

The man glared back at him, and in the wordless exchange that followed between the man and the beast, it was Royal Exile who lost his temper first. Before the man ever knew what had happened, the stallion pinned back his ears and cut out in the opposite direction. Keeping hold of the shank, the man was dragged a short distance by the powerful horse. Then realizing that he was not going to let go, Royal Exile stopped.

As soon as he got to his feet, the handler delivered a hard, swift kick into the horse's underbelly as punishment. It obviously hurt the stallion because his head dropped forward and he stood so still that for a moment it appeared as though he were holding his breath.

"Do you think your father's really hurt?" Thunderball asked, concerned.

"I hope not, but I've never seen him do that before," Freddie answered.

They watched in distress as the man yanked on the chain again, forcing Royal Exile to walk with him. The harsh sounds of hatred ran out of his mouth in the form of embittered words as he took another cigarette out of his breast pocket. Hands shaking, he lit it just as they entered Royal Exile's barn.

Freddie stared after him for a long time, feeling angry that anyone would treat his father so unkindly.

"I think it would have been a little easier if that guy would have started out by showing a little courtesy," Thunderball commented. "Royal Exile can be a handful, but he's not mean. He's just particular."

"Well, my father did lose his temper with him, and that isn't right either. Maybe it was because he was a stranger. I would have thought that someone who knew him would have come for him today," he responded, trying to take into consideration the actions of both the stallion and the handler. "I guess my father never mistreats his regular groom because his regular groom never mistreats him. I'll be glad when he comes back."

CHAPTER SIX

The End Of An Era

IT WAS NOT LONG after an evening thunderstorm had cleared that Freddie saw a strange light radiating from Royal Exile's barn. It was so faint that, at first, it gave the impression that the sun had started to rise again directly inside of the building. There were shades of yellow and orange that varied in color and formed an eerie halo above the clapboard building.

Freddie watched it suspiciously because even when all the lights were on inside his father's residence, he had never seen it look this way. Flaring his nostrils, he inhaled a strong, unpleasant odor on the night breeze, and at the same moment, he realized it was the scent of smoke. He saw the spindly fingers of fire stretch through the thin crack between the barn doors.

Sticking his nose in the air he squealed a warning long and loud. "Fire! There is a fire in Royal Exile's barn!"

He could feel the muscles throughout his body tense the way they used to just before he raced. It was followed by a rush of energy that sent him galloping across the slippery

wet grass to get closer to his father, and when he reached the end of his paddock, he cried out again.

"It's a fire! Thunderball, we have to call somebody to help him. He has to get out!"

In what seemed a single stride, Thunderball was there, and the two young stallions both began running frantically along the paddock fence, desperately hollering for help. They threw their heads back, and bucked and kicked until they created such a disturbance that even the rabbits in the surrounding shrubbery scampered toward the woods for protection.

"Just be calm fellas," Woodrow instructed as he hurried by. "I'm going to the house to get someone to help."

He was moving as fast as his sturdy legs would carry him, leaping through the fence rail as he sprinted to the main house. When he reached the front drive, he barked and barked for someone to come out, and when they did not, he scurried around to the back of the house and his calls for help reached a fevered pitch.

An aimless stream of smoke rose in the air, then rambled across the pastures, causing all of the horses within them to rustle uncomfortably. Once they were able to recognize it as their enemy, fire, they shrieked with fear and started herding themselves away from it. The broodmares called their foals to their sides and followed the lead broodmare to an isolated, dark corner of the field where they hoped the flames would not find them. Soon, all of the stallions were dashing violently along the borders of their paddocks, foaming at the mouth and sending out raging cries that one of their band was in danger.

Freddie could barely stand the helplessness he felt as he watched the yellow flickers turn to crimson heat within the building, then he heard the loud thud of Royal Exile kicking at the walls of his stall. Strangely, not a single cry was heard from him, only the determined pounding of his hooves as he tried to get free.

Fearing that he would not get out, Freddie attempted to run in a wide circle so that he could jump the fence and help him. Yet each time he tried, his hooves slipped beneath him because the ground was too wet to allow him to gain enough momentum to hoist his thick, barrel-chest over the highest board. He continued trying though, believing that each effort would be successful, until the grass turned to a slick plain of mud, and there were bloody gashes along both his shoulders and down his front legs.

By the time the farmhands came running, Freddie was so lathered that he looked like he had just finished running his toughest race. The sweat was stinging his eyes, and dripping off his belly. Still, for all of his bodily strength, he felt completely powerless. Even the drone of the approaching fire engine siren offered him little comfort because by then almost the entire barn was engulfed in flames.

"Get that horse out of there!" one of the men commanded. "He's still alive, I can hear him pacing."

In the next moment Royal Exile's regular groom was using an axe to break through the main entry because the door latch was too hot to hold. Freddie could hear him crying Royal Exile's name over and over, assuring the horse that he was about to be rescued. With his next strong swing, the smooth wood splintered apart and the vicious blaze leaped out igniting the groom's sleeve.

The young man did not seem to notice as he continued hacking away at the door, while another man used a single garden hose to put it out. As soon as the opening was wide enough to get through, the groom dropped the axe and tried to enter the barn, but the smoke was so thick that he started to choke from it. Then, one of the firemen hastily pulled him back into the fresh air so he would not suffocate.

By this time, Freddie had his muddy forelegs on the top fence board, and his head craned forward hoping to catch the first glimpse of Royal Exile emerging to safety. He heard something rustle in the tree above him and when he glanced up, he found Patches crouched on a branch watching as well. The fur was up along her back, and her eyes were so wide and glassy that Freddie could see the reflection of the burning barn in both of them.

She must have felt him looking at her, because when she met his eye her look of dread was replaced with one of absolute sympathy.

"It will be all right, Freddie," she meowed. "We have to think only good thoughts of Royal Exile right now."

The clopping of hooves caused the young stallion to turn back without responding, and what he saw made him gasp in horror. Royal Exile was running blindly toward him and there were flames rising off the round of his back and his forelegs. The stablehands were following him with buckets of water and even the fireman took his powerful water hose away from the barn and directed it at him.

The water was spraying out in all directions, resembling a thundershower that was only raining in one place, and the men were yelling for him to whoa. His groom was running alongside him, coughing and wheezing, and with one heave, he tossed the bucket of water and its contents directly onto the center of the stallion's back and put out the flames.

Freddie could smell the awful stench of burning fur as the stud suddenly dropped to the ground, and rolled in the grass. As he did this, the others were able to pour the water on his forelegs as well.

Royal Exile lay perfectly still for a moment with only his groom hovering over him. Freddie could see his sides moving up and down steadily as he gulped for air, but he still did not even whimper. It was as if he refused to show the pain because he believed that his strong body and courageous heart could endure anything. Then, he deliberately hoisted himself to his feet, turned to face the flames, reared up, and released a shrill cry as he defiantly stabbed at the distant fire with his two charred forelegs before he fell back down on the grass.

A chilling silence came over the surroundings and as Freddie hoped in vain that his father would rise again, the air was pierced with the sobbing of Royal Exile's groom. Dropping down beside the motionless horse, he wrapped his arms around its once proud neck, and let its handsome head rest in his lap until another groom came with a blanket and covered up the animal completely.

Freddie stood frozen in disbelief. Although he could hear the sound of Thunderball and Patches speaking to him, he could not make out a single word they were saying. At that moment the only thing he could think of was Rosie, and how he wanted to go to the place along the fence where they stood in the sunshine each day and find a way to forget what had just happened. He knew that all of the commotion must have frightened her away, and he wanted to go and find her if only he could get his legs to move. Then he heard her sweet, gentle voice saying his name, and as he turned, he saw that she was standing just beneath Patches. The calico had apparently led her there when Woodrow had gone for help.

Lowering his front legs to the ground, he found they were trembling so badly that he thought they were going to buckle under him. He was shaking from head to tail and the earth felt strange beneath his feet. He made himself move forward one step at a time as Rosie found her way closer. Looking at her for a long moment, he wondered if he should tell her what had just happened, but as he hid his face in the soft bow of her neck, he understood that she already knew.

Pressing himself as close as the fence would allow, he could still see the image of Royal Exile outlined against the flames, and closing his eyes, he wished that on this night he could have been blind as well.

When Royal Exile was laid to rest he was wrapped in purple satin, and placed in a varnished oak casket made especially for him. For weeks after the tragedy, so many flowers came from his fans that they formed a huge floral mound in front of his head stone. There were many visitors, particularly people who had watched Royal Exile race and wanted to pay their last respects to his memory. There was even one man who came from overseas with his daughter. She was too young to have seen Royal Exile race, but she had read about him in books and had watched his son, Rue Royale, race on television many times. For her birthday she had asked her father to bring her to America from her home in Ireland so that she could visit Freddie. Because her father was a horse trainer, and this was his only daughter, he gladly filled her request.

At first, Freddie found her a peculiar sight with her braided hair the color of carrots, and her gangly arms and legs that made her look and move more like newborn foal than a person. However, when she was introduced to him, he could not help but like the way she stroked his mane and kept repeating his name as though it had special meaning.

"Rue Royale," she would say, then she would give a giggle and say it again. It had been a long time since Freddie had heard someone use his race name, and because of her accent, it had a happy ring to it as it rolled off her tongue. She fed him peppermint candy then turned to Rosie and held out her hand for the mare to smell.

Rosie sniffed it, then filled her lungs with air and gave a relaxed sigh. The grey mare did not even twitch when the girl stroked her face, and ran her fingertip over the smooth, empty sockets of her eyes.

"She must be very kind," the girl said to her father.

"Well, how would you know that?" he questioned. He smiled so broadly when he looked at his daughter that wrinkles appeared in the corners of his eyes. Freddie could tell by the calloused, weathered skin on his hands that he was used to being outdoors.

"Because Rue Royale likes her," she replied. "And I can tell by the expression in his eyes that he is a very kind too."

Freddie's groom chuckled. "Yes," he broke in. "He does like her an awful lot. Why the two of them spend just about the whole day at the fence visiting with each other. It's good for him to have a friend because when he got here he had a tough time settling in. Racehorses like him sometimes find it hard to adjust to life on the farm because it can be very quiet after all the excitement of the track. But since he met Rosie, he doesn't seem to be lonely anymore. We all think it's nice that Freddie and Rosie are a pair."

"Freddie?" she asked. "Who's Freddie?"

The groom patted the chestnut horse on the forehead. "This is Freddie. Around here nobody calls him Rue Royale. We call him, Freddie. It's his barn name."

The girl covered her mouth with her hand and laughed heartily. "Freddie," she murmured. "Freddie, I like that name."

That night when Freddie lay down to sleep, he thought of the girl with the hair the color of carrots, and about the way she touched him so gently, as well as how she knew that Rosie was nice and so important to him. He thought about the way that her father had brought her so many miles to visit and lay flowers at his sire's grave, and he decided that she must be very kind too.

Unlike Royal Exile, Freddie did not mistrust people. Rather, he always tried to find something to like about them. It was true that they did not always understand horses, but then there were horses that did not always understand them either. The most Freddie had ever expected was for them to at least try to understand him, and he would return the courtesy. However, what had happened to Royal Exile was unfair. It was almost as though his worst fear of being dependent on a human had come true, and that by the carelessness of the groom smoking a cigarette in the barn, he had been forced to pay with his life.

Nestling into the thick bed of straw in his stall, Freddie closed his eyes and tried not to think of how horrible his father's last moments must have been—the fear and defenselessness Royal Exile must have faced when he looked at the fury of the flames, knowing that they could consume him just like they could wood or straw. As the chestnut stallion drifted off into a deep slumber, he remembered Patches' advice, and purposely made himself think of the good memories he had of his sire instead.

Royal Exile had always seemed the immovable mountain, steadfast and dignified, with a voice so deep that it could have been made of thunder. Freddie could still picture the stallion's disapproving gaze on the first day Freddie had met him and the way he had been so impatient when Freddie had bowed his head.

"Don't bow your head!" he had told him. "A racehorse should be proud and confident. His head should never hang down."

His words sounded so real that Freddie was startled out of his sleep. He looked around the barn, then listened a moment, but did not hear anything but the relaxed, heavy breathing of the other stallions.

Resting his head in the straw again, he felt a terrible yearning in his heart as he realized that these few memories were all that he could cherish for the rest of his life.

"Oh, Father," he whispered sleepily. "I miss you so much."

He could feel his body relaxing as he gave way to sleep, and he tried once more to remember. He could vividly make out the pictures of his childhood as he recalled the lush green grass of the pasture, and the huge oak tree that loomed in the center of it. He could recall how enormous the world seemed then, and how he used to race against Thunderball and imagine he was as great a racehorse as Royal Exile.

"How old are you?" Freddie heard the horse ask.

Freddie knew that he was dreaming because he could see himself as a young foal looking up at the awesome sight of his father.

"I'm five months old," he answered.

"You run very fast for your age. Your stride will be long, take advantage of that. Remember to keep your head up and stretch out as far as you can when you run. That will keep you in front when a race comes down to the wire."

All at once, Freddie's dream shifted and he found himself on the home stretch of Churchill Downs. He could see the majestic twin spires over the grandstand and hear the sound of the people cheering him on. He was running in the Kentucky Derby again, only this time instead of facing Revolver, he was running all by himself. There was no other horse on the track except Royal Exile, who stood proudly on the other side of the finish line.

Just like before, Freddie dug down deep into his heart and stretched his head out the way his father had told him. Only this time, the reward was not beating a rival like Revolver; it was living up to the expectations he had of himself and having his father feel proud of the individual he had become.

With his first stride across the finish line, Freddie could see the exhilaration in Royal Exile's eyes. The sun was shining on his handsome face, and the wind was whipping through his thick mane. He took a step nearer to son, then stopped and nodded his head approvingly.

"Yours is the blood of champions. As long as you remember that, I will never be forgotten," he said clearly and very kindly. Then he turned and galloped off into the distance, and Freddie felt himself starting to wake.

He opened his eyes a slit, and when he saw that it was still night and that he had only been asleep a short time, he shut them again.

"I promise you, Father, I will remember you forever," he murmured, then fell back to sleep.

CHAPTER SEVEN

A New Beginning

FREDDIE ROSE BEFORE the sun the next morning, feeling re-
freshed and content. He felt a sense of delight at the still
slumbering world around him as though a single night had
turned it into something splendid and perfect.

Peering out his window, he watched a bluebird sweep
through the sky, and was taken by the grace with which it
was able to glide through the air using its feathered wings.
He thought of the many creatures that lived on the earth,
how each one was unique, and he knew that this was what
made them so special. Up until that morning, he had never
considered the idea that true character and beauty was defined not by how much one resembled another, but by the way
in which they differed.

Turning his sights to the foundation of ash that had once
been Royal Exile's barn, he thought of the dream he had the
night before. He knew that what he had seen was only a wish
fulfilled by sleep, but it gave him the feeling that life was still
rewarding, even if his father would no longer be there to
share it with him.

He munched down his breakfast in silence and when he was turned out, he ran around his paddock, throwing his head and kicking out his legs as playfully as when he was a foal. He stopped only to listen to the singing of the birds, then he whinnied a reply and galloped out again. It was too early for Rosie to be there, so while Freddie waited for her, he rolled in the soft grass and finally settled down to graze.

Although the sun was as bright as it had been the day before, this day was special, and he knew it. It was nothing he could put into words. It was just a feeling he had, and when he saw Romantic Myth being led down the lane by a stable hand, he knew the reason.

Mother and son seldom had a chance to talk these days, because Freddie resided with the stallions and Romantic Myth with the broodmares. However, when the farrier came to put shoes on her, she was taken by Freddie's paddock on the way to the shoeing area, and her groom was always kind enough to let them have a visit.

Even at a distance, Freddie could see the lines of sadness on her face, and her large kind eyes seemed to droop, causing her to look much older than her years. Yet despite her grief, her blood-bay coat reflected a healthy sheen in the daylight, and her unhurried gait still showed the refined grace and sense of purpose she had always possessed.

Still, she was a much older Romantic Myth than he had seen before. The tragedy of Royal Exile left her with a deep sorrow in her heart. A tear showed in her eye as she looked back at her son, but when she started to speak, her voice was rich with strength and understanding.

"I'm sorry that you had to see what happened to your Father, Freddie. I know it's not the way he would want for you to remember him," she said.

"He was brave until the end, Mother," Freddie responded. "That is what I remember."

A warm wind rose rustling the leaves in the trees as it blew. It still carried the scent of burnt wood, and as it ruffled Romantic Myth's dark mane, she turned her head and looked at what was left of Royal Exile's barn.

"You must not be angry with the groom for his carelessness. He did not intend to cause your father's death," she explained. "Sometimes something so innocent can bring terrible consequences. I'm sure he had no idea that his cigarette would cause such a terrible fire."

Freddie hesitated to reply as the image of the burning building flashed in his mind as she spoke. His first inclination was to say something hurtful about the incident, but then he remembered what Patches had told him. He must think good thoughts about his father.

"Do you understand, Freddie?" Romantic Myth asked kindly. "When you hold anger in your heart, the only one who suffers is you. None of us are perfect—not even humans."

"That does not make the groom's carelessness right," he replied. "Every man and animal may not be perfect, but that does not give them the right to be so irresponsible that it would harm another."

Romantic Myth regretfully shook her head, then looked straight into her son's eyes as she spoke. "No, Freddie, he is responsible for his actions, and because of that, he is also the one who must live with the guilt. Your anger toward him will amount to nothing, but your compassion for his burden will. It is nothing more than replacing vengefulness with forgiveness, because one day you too might be in need of the same consideration."

Freddie nodded. "I understand," he answered. "Mother?"

"Yes, Freddie."

"I had a beautiful dream about my father last night," he told her. "I dreamed that I saw him, and he talked with me. It seemed so real, almost as if it was not a dream at all and he was still alive."

"He is alive, Freddie," she answered, her voice suddenly hopeful. "He is alive in you and all the rest of his line. And your dream is real too. It is as real as you believe it to be. If Royal Exile lives in your memory, then that is enough. You were his best son on the track, so don't forget that. The things you accomplished might be behind you now, but they were important and true to the blood of your ancestors. The bloodline you pass on is the bloodline of greatness."

As she finished her sentence, her groom stroked her forehead, and she knew it was time for her to go. "Be brave now, son," she told him. "And remember that I am always here for you."

"Yes, Mother," he replied, wishing she did not have to go so soon. "I love you very much."

"I love you too, Freddie," she answered, then continued on her way.

Freddie said very little the remainder of that day—even to Rosie. His thoughts were far away as he remembered the first years of his life. He let the remembrances fill his mind, and while they did not come in any particular order, each one had a special place in his heart. Some of them were quite happy ones of places and friends who had drifted in and out of his life. Others were of events that did not seem so good when they had happened, but had become dear to him with the passage of time. Then there were those recollections that were so extraordinary that they made his heart swell with joy.

He was glad that at sunset no one came to take him or Rosie indoors. The fresh air and open pasture better suited his mood than the barn, and when the full moon showered the farm with pale light, it made him feel as though a new world was entirely within his reach.

"Rosie, did you ever wonder what it is like to race?" he asked.

Rosie lifted her head and her ears twitched. "Oh, yes," she answered enthusiastically. "I think it must be scary and exciting at the same time. Just once I would like to know what it feels like to extend my legs and go as fast as they would carry me, and for a single stride I would be like all the other horses. Tell me Fred, is it wonderful?"

"Yes, Rosie, it is more wonderful than I can describe," he replied. "I would like to show how it feels, if you will trust me."

"I will, Fred."

At that, Freddie backed up, and took a running start to jump the fence. It had not rained for days, so the ground stayed firm beneath him and he was able to leap over on his first try. He startled Rosie when his hooves touched down beside her, then he heard her laugh as she realized what he had done.

"They will be angry if they find you here," she said cautiously. "I'm afraid that if they see that you've done it a second time, they might separate us for good."

Freddie shrugged. "You might be right. Do you want me to go back?"

"Yes," she answered, "but I want to run like a racehorse just once before you do."

The chestnut stallion gave her big smile. "All right. Just stay at my side, and no matter how much you want to stop, don't until I say so. All right?"

"All right," the grey mare answered bravely.

Freddie started at an easy trot and with each step increased the pace until he and Rosie were at a brisk canter. He kept an eye on her all the time to be certain that she was right by his side. Noticing that her nostrils were flared and her mouth very tense, he did not want to go any faster until he was sure that she felt confident.

Rosie's gait was smooth and unhurried as she flung her legs out farther and farther until she was almost breezing along. She said nothing to Freddie, never questioning whether there was an obstacle in her way, and he realized just how much faith she had in him.

They completed one circle around the paddock, and as they neared the starting point, it was Rosie not Freddie who quickened her step. She did it as though she was pushing through an invisible barrier she had always feared.

The two thoroughbreds rounded the paddock again, this time at a full gallop. The ground beneath them rumbled and clumps of grass flew out behind them with each thrilling stride. Bravely inching in front of Freddie, Rosie laughed a lighthearted laugh between hasty breaths.

"Have you ever had so much fun?" Freddie asked, catching his wind and laughing with her.

"No, Fred," Rosie answered. "I think this is what freedom feels like. This has been the best summer of my life. Thank you for this."

When summer ended that year, Rosie was able to picture the green leaves of the trees as they changed to vibrant colors of yellow, red, and orange through Freddie's descriptions of them. Soon, the once warm wind announced the chill that led to the winter snows, and the seasons continued to turn until it was summer all over again, and Rosie was being escorted to the foaling barn.

Her once tidy conformation was now rounded with the presence of a baby horse. Her ankles were so swollen that her slim pasterns looked like they would touch the ground if she were forced to wait one more day to birth.

Leaving Freddie with the worrisome task of waiting for the arrival of their first offspring, Rosie trudged so slowly up the road that her hooves could have been made of cement. But that mattered little to Freddie, all he wanted was for them to be reunited as soon as possible. He knew what Rosie did not: because she could not see, her foal would be given over to a nursemare to raise. However sad it made him to think about it, he understood that it was for the best. Young horses could be very unpredictable, and the worry of not knowing what it was doing at all times would be a terrible strain on both Rosie and her baby. Freddie would be sure to explain that to Rosie when the time came, and he would make it absolutely clear that it was through no fault of her own that their foal was with another.

When Rosie was turned loose in a foaling box deep with clean straw, she found her way over to the feed bin and sniffed the hay, but did not eat any of it. Her large, warm belly was jiggling with new life, and each time the concealed, miniature hoof pressed into her side, she groaned uncomfortably at the feel of it.

"You're going to be fine, Mama," the vet told her, as he touched his hand to her stomach and smiled. "It won't be long now."

Knowing that a mare does not like to foal if someone is watching, he patted her sweaty chest then left her alone. Going into a nearby office, he watched her through a window instead. Since this was her first foal, she might need his help to birth it.

As the hours ticked by, Rosie lay down on her side, trying to find restful moments between the jerks of her body. When the doctor saw that she had started to tremble, he went to her side and waited for the first glimpse of the new foal.

It seemed as if a very long time had passed, but within a few minutes the wobbling legs of a baby horse danced into a new world, and Rosie was stretched out quietly with her head down on the straw. Since she could not see it, she did not know that it was a filly whose black coat would one day be as grey as her own. Nor could she watch as it lifted its downy soft nostrils to breathe in its first sample of air.

"Does it have eyes?" she questioned, but to the veterinarian it only sounded like a tired nicker.

"There, there, Mama," he soothed. "Your filly is strong, and her bones are very correct. And Mama, you don't have to worry. She has the biggest, kindest eyes I have ever seen. Why, they are even prettier than her father's. I'm sure Freddie will be very proud."

As if she could understand his every word, Rosie sighed then began to stir nervously at the uncertain movements of the newborn horse. More than anything, she feared that she might accidently hurt it with her slightest move.

"Easy now," the vet comforted. "She's just trying to find her legs, so give her a minute."

Rosie heard the vet laugh, then listened to the straw rustle with small steps.

"Her name will be Baroness, is that all right?" he questioned.

Rosie sighed again, and a moment later her filly was taken to another stall where an old nursemare, Flyspeck, was waiting to assume her care.

CHAPTER EIGHT

Keeneland

THE FIRST THING Baroness noticed was the tension in the air as she was led into the sales pavilion. Fourteen months had gone by since her birth, and she was now a yearling. It was July, and she found herself at one of the most prestigious horse sales in the country, the Keeneland Yearling Sale.

She stood quietly with a number taped on her hip designating her place in the sale. The sheen of her charcoal coat beamed beneath the overhead lights as she waited to be brought out onto the auction ring. She listened with some misgivings to the loud words of the auctioneer as he slurred them together to create a language she could not understand. It was a sound so harsh that it made her want to run from it. Then, there were the many human voices fading in and out, and although they were not quite as loud as the announcer, they still gave her reason to fret.

Of course she had only lived little more than year in the world, but she knew exactly what was happening in her young life. She was at the lovely Keeneland Racecourse in the rolling green hills of Lexington, Kentucky. From the time she was a foal in the broodmare pasture, she had been told by her nursemare that if she was lucky, this was the sale where she would be purchased.

The barn area was spacious and clean, and all of the people she had seen there, from the handlers to the potential buyers, were all very kind and seemed to know a great deal about horses.

Throughout the last week, many of them had come to the barn to look at the yearlings being offered. Baroness had watched the horses on either side of her being previewed often, but unlike them, she had only been taken out once or twice. Sometimes from the way they spoke about her, she was not sure if they wanted to see her because they were interested in buying her, or because they wanted to view one of the first offspring sired by Rue Royale.

Once she had overheard one of the stablehands comment that she probably would not sell for much money, if she sold at all. The farm where she came from had only placed the minimum reserve price on her to recover their expenses for sales preparation, transportation charges, and daily feeding costs. She remembered the tiny quiver she felt in her stomach when they said that they were surprised she was even there because her dam was unraced. Although her sire was a champion runner, he had not yet proven his value as a stud.

"The way I heard it, it wasn't a planned breeding," one of them had said to the other. "The stallion jumped the fence."

Baroness felt a terrible hollow feeling within her and tried to ignore their comments by retreating to the corner of her stall with her back turned. All her life she had known that she was not the same as the other thoroughbreds she was brought up with because unlike them, she did not have a sleek, well-bred broodmare to raise her. Instead, she was raised by a nursemare with a fuzzy white coat that had thousands of red flecks all over it, which was why she was affectionately called Flyspeck.

Since she had spent most of her life caring for orphaned foals, Flyspeck did not have any race stories to share with Baroness, and she did not gallop along the fence with her either. Rather, she was quiet and nice, always assuring Baroness that she was loved for who she was, not whom she was born.

Naturally, there were always rumors amongst the foals that Baroness' mother had been the blind mare in the pasture next to the stallion, Rue Royale, but not even Baroness had believed them until she saw the pedigree on the brass name plate of her halter. Only then did she wonder what her mother had been like.

She remembered passing by her a few times on her way to or from the veterinarian or the farrier. She recalled the peculiar sight of her sculptured face that would have been very beautiful were it not for the fur-covered sockets where the eyes should have been. And what stood out the most in Baroness' mind was that each time Baroness went by her, the blind mare would kindly ask Flyspeck how Baroness was getting along, as did the chestnut stallion, Rue Royale.

While it seemed a very long time ago, there was something about the experience that seemed very important to her now. Although neither the stallion nor the mare had addressed her directly, somehow Baroness always knew that she was special to them both. She was not sure how she knew. Perhaps she had realized it with a single gesture from the grey or from the gentle look in the eyes of the chestnut, but it was very clear. It was also apparent from a very young age that she could not count on her bloodlines to make her great. She had to rely on herself. Whether she was purchased at this sale or not, she was determined to prove herself as a racehorse.

There was no doubt that she could run faster than the other foals, but it was not courage that made her stride out ahead of them. It was fear. Baroness felt afraid when she ran — afraid in a way she could not explain. At that very moment as she looked upon the auction ring, she wished she could run away from it as well. More than anything, she was terrified that not one of all the people who would look at her would want to take her home, and she would never even have the chance to race.

As she was led into the roped area with the three men in the raised booth behind her, Baroness' eyes became so strangely enlarged that the white showed around them. Pricking up her ears, she took a deep breath and screeched so loud that she could not even believe that the sound had come from her.

Row after row of seats were filled with people, all them looking at her with vague disinterest. Scanning their faces, Baroness did not see a single person she recognized. She whinnied again, even louder, only this time it was a cry for friendship. She wanted desperately to feel wanted by someone because the thought that she was not good enough to be there was filling her mind.

Moving backward, she tried to turn to get away, but the handler faced her forward again. Unable to make herself look into the faces of the others, Baroness fixed her eyes on the very back row, and saw the face of a young girl that seemed to stand out from all the others. She remembered it because her skin was flawlessly white making her blazing, carrot-colored hair that much brighter. She was one of the few people that had come to visit the filly in the stables, and she had made a comment about having once seen the blind mare next to Rue Royale's paddock. She had kindly stroked Baroness' mane and spoke softly to her, and when Baroness rubbed her head on the girl's shoulder, she laughed sweetly and patted the side of the filly's face.

The happy feeling of this recollection vanished instantly as she shifted her gaze to the rest of the people seated stiffly in their chairs, and she felt a jolt of panic. The voice over the loud speaker kept repeating her hip number and her sire's name, but it did not matter how many times it was called, Baroness knew that not one of them was going to make a bid on her.

She felt suddenly helpless, and her urge to run away was so strong that her long straight legs began to prance in place. When the handler jerked on the shank to stop her, she whinnied as loud as before, but this time it was to ask someone to please, please make an offer on her. Then, she looked at the pale-skinned girl, and neighed directly at her once, then twice, then three times.

The girl's eyes widened, and she stood and tried to walk toward her, but the man beside her made her sit back down.

"But she's talking to me," the girl said. "Father, she is talking right to me."

"Don't be imagining things," he answered, kindly patting her hand. "Just sit quietly, you haven't the money to buy her."

She wilted back in her chair, but even as Baroness was being led away, the girl's smooth, young face reflected only sympathy and understanding for what the filly must be feeling.

Baroness was handed off to a groom who took her back through the barn area. She wished he would have patted her or said something to make her feel better, because at that moment, she felt like no one in the world cared about her. She knew how important this sale was because it would determine her entire future. She needed to have a good owner who would give her the opportunity to race. She had heard many stories of talented horses who were not sent to the right trainer and sometimes raced when they should not have, and they ended up getting hurt. Baroness did not want that to happen to her, and she did not want to end up doing circles in a sand arena all day long like the show horses. She wanted to race the way her father had raced, even if it was the hardest thing she ever did.

Her halter was removed, and she rolled in the fresh straw of her stall. Wiggling around, she scratched her back then flopped over and rubbed the side of her face where the halter had been. She tried not to think of how discouraged she was at not being bought by someone, especially since she knew that the fillies on either side of her had sold for quite a high price.

Now she felt ashamed to even talk to them. She was afraid they would tease her, but then she reasoned that no horse ever died from an insult. She decided that they had both been nice to her before the auction, so there was no reason why they would not be nice to her again. She would make herself talk to them, even if she felt anxious about it.

"I'll teach myself to be brave," she told herself. "I'll make myself face things I want to hide from."

Shaking the straw from her back, Baroness poked her head out of the stall and nickered. In a moment, the filly beside her looked out and smiled. She had very large eyes with long lashes, and there was a perfect blaze down her nose.

"I heard the news and I'm sorry, Baroness," she said. "There are so many of us at these sales that it's hard to predict which of us will be sold and which won't. My mother explained it to me a long time ago so that I would understand when I got here. She said that the race market changes from year to year, and some bloodlines bring higher prices than others."

Baroness nodded and made herself smile back at the filly. "I know," she said, trying not to sound upset.

"It's especially hard if you are one of the first of your sire's crop, because nobody knows how his offspring will run."

Baroness shrugged and stared down at the ground. "They'll never find out if they don't give us the chance."

Just then the filly on the other side of Baroness' stall stretched her neck out far enough to nuzzle Baroness on the cheek. Her name was Jenny Mae, and she had been bought by a very well-known family in racing and was going to be sent overseas to Ireland.

"Don't feel bad, Baroness," she said, giving her a friendly nip on the nose. "Sometimes on the last day of the auction, they'll drop the price just so they can make a sale, so maybe you'll get a home that way."

"It might happen, but then what kind of an owner will I get if they could not afford me from the start," she commented, keeping her head down.

"Maybe the best kind," the first filly added. "Maybe you'll get the kind of owner who isn't worried about money, but will give you a good home just because they like you. Personally, I hear all this talk about money, but I don't even know what it is."

"Me neither," Jenny Mae added with a nicker. "But people talk about it like it's the most important thing in the world."

Baroness lifted her head and looked at them both. "That's only because it's the color of alfalfa hay," she said flatly, and disappeared back into her stall.

CHAPTER NINE

Baroness Gets Her Wish

THE SALE ENDED, and Baroness watched as one by one the yearlings were loaded onto long transport vans. The horses wore
padded white standing wraps on all four legs to protect their
delicate young tendons while they were being hauled. Jenny
Mae and the other filly were now gone, and the sales staff and
the horse handlers were packing up their belongings as well,
so by the end of the day the backside of Keeneland Racecourse
looked almost deserted.

As night set in, the surroundings grew hauntingly quiet,
and Baroness realized that she was all alone in the darkness.
With the exception of the night watchman who walked down
the shedrow every now and then, the filly felt as if she was the
only horse left on the grounds. She tried her best to go to
sleep, but the slightest sound, from the cricket's chirp to the
summer breeze that rustled the tree branches, kept her from
her slumber.

She spent the restless hours sending out worried calls, hoping that another horse would answer. When she finally did
start to nap, she had the same nightmare over and over

again—when the sun came up, no one would ever come back to get her.

She tried to reason with herself that such a thing could not happen, that she had to be important to somebody. But when the anxiety was too much for her to take, she would whinny as loud as she could and was always thankful when a faint reply drifted over to her from a distant barn.

Morning came at last, and Baroness was overjoyed at the sight of her groom coming down the shedrow with her breakfast. She nuzzled him happily when he placed her feed bucket in the stall and hung her hay net on the side of the doorway.

Running his hand across her chest, he saw she was a bit sweaty, and he knew she was feeling uneasy, so he stayed with her for a time, stroking her forehead and speaking to her softly. When she finished her meal, he brushed her from head to toe, and rubbed the sheen into her coat with a towel before he started putting on her leg wraps.

Baroness craned her neck around and watched with interest as he wrapped her back legs first. He was careful to apply each bandage so that it was snug enough to stay on, but not so tight as to be uncomfortable. When he had done the same to her front legs, he then arranged her forelock so that it lay neatly in the center of her forehead.

"Your pasterns are a little long anyway," he commented as if he knew something she did not. "I think the soft grass where you are going will suit you better than the dirt here in America."

Baroness looked at him questioningly, and he started to say something more, but was distracted by two people walking up the shedrow.

"She's all ready for you," the groom said, and Baroness looked up to find the same young girl she had called to in the sales pavilion the day before. Her orange hair was pulled back away from her face, and as the filly looked at her more closely, she noticed that her green eyes were bright with expectation.

"She needs a little time to grow into herself," the groom went on. "Look at how big her feet are, and her pasterns, well, you can see for yourself that they are a little long. I've only worked with this filly a short time, but I can tell you that she's not like the others. It's a strange thing, but she seems to have this deep fear inside of her, like she's afraid of life. But when you handle her, it's obvious that she has a good mind and tries very hard to understand what is expected of her. I think if she had someone to believe in her and build her confidence more, she could really be a runner. Once you teach her something, she remembers it forever."

The girl reached out her hand and ran it along Baroness' neck then down her shoulder. Normally, Baroness would have shied away from a stranger touching her with such familiarity. Yet there was such gentleness in the girl's manner that she could not help but enjoy it, especially after such a lonely night.

"We'll be the best of friends," she replied, then looked over at the older man who was with her. "Thank you for giving me this chance, Father."

The man shook his head as his eyes followed the lines of Baroness' back. "Tiffany O'Connell, you may be my only child, but I have to tell you that if your dear mother was alive today, she'd not have any part of this."

He placed his hand to his brow and looked at the groom doubtfully.

"I did the worst possible thing," he told him. "Two years ago, for Tiffany's fourteenth birthday, I brought her over from Ireland to visit her favorite horse, Rue Royale. Do you know of him?"

The groom nodded. "Sure I do, but around the farm we call him Freddie."

"That's right, Freddie was his name indeed," Mr. O'Connell went on. "Well, Tiffany not only took a liking to Freddie, but to the blind mare next him named Rosie. So when we arrived here and she saw that this filly was their offspring, Tiffany spent all of her inheritance to buy the creature."

Tiffany leaned over and kissed Mr. O'Connell on the cheek. "She's not a creature, she's the best horse in the world."

Her father could not resist her affection, but the clouded look in his eyes remained. "Daughter, I'm afraid you and this filly will have to convince me of that."

"Father, you have given me the best gift ever, and I know that Baroness will love living in Ireland," she replied, holding out a carrot to the horse.

Baroness gnawed on it at first, then took a bite. Keeping her eye on the girl, she munched it down, then let out a contented sigh that made Tiffany giggle.

"She'll make us proud if we believe in her," she said, attaching the shank to the halter and taking her out of the stall. "I'm certain of that. Baroness will be better than anyone realizes."

CHAPTER TEN

The Emerald Isle

BARONESS HAPPILY SETTLED into her new home in Ireland. Along with Jenny Mae, she had endured the long journey on the airplane and found herself in a small kingdom of thoroughbreds in the County Kildare.

They called Ireland the Emerald Isle, but Baroness thought the terrain resembled Kentucky in many ways. The gentle sloping hillsides seemed to stretch out so far that they appeared to be touching the horizon. They were so smooth and green and soft that Baroness thought that they would break away beneath her if she set a hoof on them.

The days were brisk and moist, and with the exception of an occasional warm afternoon, it seldom became uncomfortably hot. The surroundings were quite peaceful, and all of the people on the farm seemed to have a natural ability to understand and work with horses. This was particularly true of Tiffany O'Connell. She came to the yearling pasture the first morning at sunrise and called for Baroness to come to her. As soon as she did, she was rewarded with a carrot. Every morning thereafter, Tiffany found Baroness waiting for her at the pasture gate.

At the end of the day, when Tiffany was finished working the other horses and cleaning their stalls, she would come to see Baroness again. It was usually early enough—unless it was raining, which it did quite often in Ireland—that Tiffany and Baroness could go for a walk. They would stroll down the lane lined on either side with tidy flowerbeds, past the old original stone outbuildings, then through a field of grazing sheep and another full of cattle, until they reached a small pond. It was a long enough walk that by the time they reached the pond, Baroness would treat herself to a drink of cool water then munch on the carrots or apple that Tiffany brought especially for her.

The young girl would tell the filly all she had done that day, and while Baroness did not understand every word, she was able to understand what she was speaking about by the tone of her voice. She knew when Tiffany was talking about horses or riding because her voice became very excited and her words very short. When she would mention one particular horse, a look of hidden fear would show in her eyes and her mannerisms would become very tense. He was called Savage, and all of the yearlings knew who he was. They had been told about him by the other horses. He was a rogue who hated people and horses so much that he would kill either of them if given the chance.

When he galloped by the yearling pasture on his way to training each morning, he would snort and throw his head, then try to bite Tiffany's foot. She would tap him between the ears with her crop, and he would respond by darting to one side in an attempt to unseat her, or worse, he would try to run her into the fence or a nearby horse. Baroness would watch wide-eyed at his antics, wondering all the while how he could be so mean to Tiffany when she was such a kind person.

At other times, Tiffany spoke to Baroness about her own mother who had died when the girl was just a baby. She told the filly she understood how lonely it must have been for her not to know her real mother because Tiffany had not known her real mother either. Then she would cry softly, and the young horse would stay very near to her until her tears stopped. In all her life, Baroness had never felt so close to anyone as she did to Tiffany, and she wished she could find a way to express to her how happy she was to have her as an owner.

Then on one cloudy afternoon, Tiffany did not come at her regular time, and Baroness feared that Savage had finally gotten out of control. The horse had become very fit from all his training, and the stronger he got physically, the more unruly he became. Nervously pacing back and forth in front of the gate, Baroness tried to think only good thoughts. She did not even want to consider that perhaps Savage had harmed the girl. However, the longer she looked up the empty lane in the direction that Tiffany usually came, the more impossible it was for her to deny that something terrible must have happened.

The feed truck came and went, but Baroness was too worried to eat. The sky was starting to blacken with a storm, and she could smell the coming rain as she took in a deep breath and exhaled with a snort. When there was barely any light left, the raindrops began to fall, and Baroness neighed a desperate call to her missing friend, but was answered only by a chilly wind blowing in her face. Normally, she would have turned her back to it or huddled with the rest of the yearlings for warmth, but that would mean that she would have to give up her view of the road and would not be able to see if Tiffany was coming.

Soon the few raindrops were followed by lightning and thunder. Each time there was a flash of light, Baroness would shudder at the sight of the ghostly shadows it cast around her, and the thunder that followed made her stomach hollow with fear. The rain came down in torrents, and soon the water was dripping down her legs and creating a puddle beneath her feet. She tried to move but found that the ground around her hooves had sunken into mud holes.

"Baroness, you should come over here with us. It's warmer," Jenny Mae called to her.

"Yes, Baroness, the wind is picking up, and you'll catch a chill if you stand there all by yourself," another filly added.

Baroness looked over her shoulder at them, then stared back up the lane. "I'm waiting for someone," she replied. "I know she'll be here any time."

"If you're waiting for you're lass, she's surely not coming out in this weather," a third filly responded. "This is a big storm, and you can rest assured she's inside where it's cozy and warm. Forget about her for now."

Baroness lowered her head and watched the water trickle down her forelegs. She was trembling from the cold rain and wind, yet it was nothing compared to her missing Tiffany.

"I suppose you're right," she mumbled, using all her strength to lift her big hoof out of the mud. When she tried to pull the other one out, it stuck, so she yanked with such force that she fell backward when it finally came loose.

Hitting the wet grass with a thud, she could hear the giggling of the other fillies behind her. Making herself stand, she self-consciously shuffled over to them, and with a look of embarrassment still on her face, she turned her back to the wind.

It was still misting the next morning when another farmhand came out to the field to check the yearlings. Baroness reluctantly allowed him to examine her wet legs and run his hand over her muddy coat to be sure that she had not been injured during the storm. She shivered at the strangeness of his touch as he lifted her front hoof. His hand felt heavier than Tiffany's, and her first reaction was to jerk it away from him despite his tight hold.

Sensing her reluctance, he released it then proceeded to look at the rest of the fillies in the same manner. Baroness purposely allowed them to herd between her and farmhand because she did not want him to touch her again.

When the horses in training hit the turf that morning, Baroness ran to fence, hoping to see Tiffany gallop by. Waiting anxiously, she stuck her head between the boards the way she always did, so she could see better. She liked the sight of the horses rushing at her with their legs stretched out and their necks rounded down, but more than that, she especially liked that she could hear the rumble of their hooves long before they came into view. It started as a soft muffled sound, one that only the keen hearing of a horse could pick up, but to Baroness it sounded like her own heartbeat.

Listening to the steady rhythm of their strides, she saw six oncoming horses with their noses pointed forward and their tails swishing behind them. They jogged along in pairs, each spaced a safe distance apart, but still their muscular young frames were an impressive image moving along the emerald green line of the grass that sliced through the misty grey horizon.

Baroness could usually pick out Tiffany right away. She could tell which rider she was by her mannerisms, because her back appeared straight yet flexible, and her hands remained very still and soft on the reins. Only on this morning, much to Baroness' dismay, the girl was not visible in the group. Savage was there, but it was not Tiffany on his back. She was able to make out his burning eyes and arrogant face. He was such an intimidating figure that Baroness cowered from him.

Pulling her head back, the tip of her nose rested on the third board of the fence, and her eyes and ears were partially concealed by the fourth. The impact of Savage's hooves against the ground grew louder and louder, until it was more fierce than the thunder from the previous night's storm. A moment later, the yearling could hear his heavy breathing as he ran in front of her and sneered.

Baroness' neck shrunk into her shoulders and she held her breath. She wished she had the nerve to tell him that she meant him no harm, that she only wanted to see if Tiffany was there. As she looked up at his rider, she saw an older, stronger man, and she knew it was useless.

Baroness' ears lowered, and not wanting to give up hope, she nickered timidly, as if to politely ask where Tiffany was. Instantly, Savage's painted red nostrils flared and he gave her a low, disdainful grunt that made her wilt in her place. She watched bewildered as the horses continued on their way. When they were almost out of sight, she whinnied once more then dropped her head in disappointment. Tiffany would

probably not come that afternoon either, she thought to herself as she slowly walked back to rejoin her band.

CHAPTER ELEVEN

A Christmas Gift
For Baroness

IT WAS A BITTER WINTER for Baroness that year. There was freezing rain that sometimes lasted for days at a time, and the drops were so big that they felt like pebbles pelting her coat. The wind blew in harsh flurries, and the sun only occasionally peeked out from the clouds to shed a dim light on the dreary surroundings.

The moon had grown full many times since the last time Baroness had seen Tiffany, and while the daylight hours grew shorter with the onset of winter, they seemed much longer for Baroness because she never forgot the girl who used to make her feel so very special.

Savage had gone on to race in England and was undefeated, but he had also thrown his jockeys in fits of temper and seriously injured his groom with his hooves and teeth for no reason at all. The stories of his roguishness spread throughout the farm, and those who had known him swore that he had gone completely insane.

As for Baroness, she was certain that Tiffany had fallen victim to his malice. It had been so long since the filly had seen the young girl that their afternoons at the pond together seemed as distant as her recollections of being a foal in America. She worried that if her friend never returned, her dreams of becoming a racehorse would be gone along with her.

For the second time in her life, Baroness watched as a pine tree was chopped down and dragged from the woods into the house. It was placed in the front picture window and at night it was radiant with colorful lights and beautiful Christmas decorations that were visible as far away as the yearling pasture. This was a happy time of year when lighted candles were placed on windowsills and friends and family would gather together to sing holiday songs and enjoy each other's company. It was during this season of joy and giving that Baroness received one of the best gifts of her life.

She knew that something special was going to happen on Christmas Day, when Tiffany's father brought her from the pasture into the barn. He curried her coat and brushed her mane, then took a damp cloth and wiped the green ring she had around her mouth from eating the wet grass. His movements were slow and gentle enough that Baroness almost dozed off before he was finished, and when he looked at her, his eyes welled with tears. Baroness had never seen such an emotional expression on his weathered face, and she offered a faint nicker to comfort him as he led her out of the barn and up the drive. After tying her near the porch of the back entrance of the main house, he went inside.

Peering through the window in front of her, Baroness could see the people milling about inside and could hear their melodic voices singing along with a piano. She did not know what to expect, so she waited quietly with her head up, her ears twitching every time the singers reached a high note.

She caught glimpses of colorfully dressed people moving by, then she saw the strangest thing. It was an odd-looking chair that rolled in front of the glass like a feedcart and stopped. Baroness' eyes grew wide with surprise, yet she remained perfectly still as she realized that the person seated in it was Tiffany.

The girl waved at the filly, who whinnied so loud that Tiffany burst into laughter. The horse took a hasty step to reach her, but her lead rope prevented her from going very far. Still wearing a smile, Tiffany disappeared from view, then reappeared on the back steps. She was still seated in the moving chair.

Refusing her father's help, Tiffany rolled herself down a temporary ramp set up over the stairs, and stopped in front of Baroness. The filly was so happy to see her that she gave her a playful nip on her hair. Then, noticing a scar on the side of her head, Baroness sniffed it curiously before touching it with her fuzzy lips.

"It's not something to eat," Tiffany told her, and using her chair as a brace, she rose to her feet.

"Careful now," her father cautioned. "This is your first day home. Don't try to do too much."

The girl shot him a prideful glance. "I am fine," she said. "I just want to see my filly."

She took a weakened step forward, then took another. At first Baroness was alarmed by the way she could hardly use her legs. This was not at all the way she remembered her. Mr. O'Connell hovered nearby with his arms held out in case she fell, but Tiffany did not even look at him. Rather, she kept a determined eye on the filly until she was alongside her.

Placing one hand on her withers, she leaned her weight into the horse's shoulder so that she could remain standing. Baroness sensed her need, and instead of moving away from her, she tightened her muscles so as to bear the girl's weight.

"Look at how tall you've gotten," Tiffany said, gently stroking her mane.

"She's tall enough, but her feet are still frightfully big," her father said. "She trips over herself when she walks, and she shies at everything. Why she even dodges her own shadow! If you were going to spend all your inheritance on a horse, you could have surely gotten a braver one than this."

Unaffected by her father's declaration, Tiffany pressed her face against Baroness' neck and kissed it. "I've missed you so much," she whispered to the filly. "Savage flipped on top of me, and that's why I've been gone so long. I'm getting better every day though, and I promise you that I will be the one who will train you. You and I are partners."

She moved her hand down the horse's back and Baroness' eyelids drooped halfway down. She was not bored, only content at being reunited with her dearest friend.

"We're going to have a grand time from now on," Tiffany said. "Ireland will never see a better filly grace their racecourse than yourself."

Baroness puffed out her chest and pricked up her ears. Maybe she was going to race after all, she thought hopefully.

For Baroness, the next few months were not marked by the changing of the seasons. She did not gauge the onset of winter by the barren trees or dreadfully cold temperatures, nor did she notice the bright blossoms at the first sign of spring, or the way the birds had returned to sing their sweet songs to mark the end of grey days. Rather, the passing of these months was measured by the stages of Tiffany's recovery.

When the girl first returned, she would wheel herself down the lane in her chair and sit for long hours at the fence visiting with Baroness. Sometimes she would read a book or sing songs to her to pass the time. Then one day she appeared walking with the help of wooden sticks called canes, which she held in each hand. Baroness was fascinated with them. She smelled them, nibbled on them, and even went so far as to pick up one of them in her mouth. She had scarcely seen such creations, and thought it would be impossible for a horse to have any use for them at all. Yet if they made it easier for her friend to walk, that was all that was important.

It was not long afterward that Tiffany regained enough strength to walk without the help of canes. It was apparent by her short steps that she had not regained full use of her legs, but the twinkle of pride in her eyes and her determination was making her stronger every day.

"They said I wouldn't be able to do it," she told Baroness. "But I am a month ahead of myself in recovering. I think it's you—you make me feel like I can do anything."

Baroness stood facing her, and Tiffany kissed her on the tip of her nose. They had both matured over this last year because of their care for each other. Baroness often wished that she could use more than a whinny or a nicker to make Tiffany understand how much she meant to her. She wanted speak plainly to her and tell her that she knew what it was to feel alone because Tiffany had rescued her when she felt the most alone ever. She wanted to tell her that she would never let her down, and that Tiffany could trust her never to do to her what Savage had done.

When at last it was time to start her training, Baroness had grown into a considerably bigger filly than the rest. Her frame was large and sturdy and so hard muscled that she looked more like a colt than a filly. Her legs were long and appeared much too skinny to support her weight, and the joints of her ankles looked too fragile to be attached to her clumsy-looking feet.

The mist still hung low on the grassy fields as the saddle was set in the center of her back for her first day of training. It felt odd at first because she had not had one on since just after the yearling sale. She flinched as Tiffany gradually tightened the girth. Tiffany worked slowly, partly because she did not want to make Baroness uncomfortable and partly because she was still very weak from her accident.

Placing the reins over Baroness' neck, she unbuckled the halter and gently slipped the bit in her mouth. The lanky filly chomped on the smooth, cold metal, and tried to move it around with her tongue. She kept bobbing her head as Tiffany buckled the noseband and throat latch, but never once did Baroness feel any hint of roughness from her.

Tiffany was so slow in getting Baroness tacked up that the group of horses they were supposed to exercise with left without them and her father even came to see if she needed his help.

"So you're still set on doing this?" he asked her with concern. "Tiffany, you have always had a mind of your own, and I'd be the last one to discourage you from living your dream, but even the doctor says you are not totally healed, and probably will never be as strong a rider as you once were."

Tiffany gave him a side glance as she tucked Baroness' forelock under the headband of the bridle. "This is my horse, I bought her with the money my mother left to me, and if it's the last thing I ever do, I'm going to teach her to be a racehorse."

Mr. O'Connell touched the tip of his finger to his lips, and his eyes passed over his daughter, then over to the filly standing beside her, and he shook his head. "I'd watch her if I were you," he cautioned. "She falls over her feet."

"Baroness will be good to me," she replied. "I don't know how to explain it Father, but it's as if she knows that I'm not myself."

"Maybe, but she hasn't hit the turf yet. If she ever goes down, that'll be the end of you," he continued.

Seeing that his daughter and Baroness were ready to go, he stepped forward and gave Tiffany a leg up into the saddle. "Don't push yourself, and don't lose your confidence when you see Savage."

The girl's head jerked around as she met his eye with a look of alarm. "Savage is back?" she asked.

Her father nodded. "For a time, and I don't have to tell you that he's got the memory of an elephant. He's the kind of horse that holds a grudge, so when you see him, don't look directly into his eyes. Steer your filly clear, and don't give him a reason to remember that you once made him angry."

Baroness could see Tiffany's pink cheeks drain of their color. "I will, Father, I wouldn't want anything to happen to Baroness."

"To Baroness!?" he declared. "I don't want anything to happen to you, so keep your wits about you. And if it comes down to you or this filly, let him have the filly."

CHAPTER TWELVE

Racing at the Curragh

THE SUN PEEKED THROUGH the mist as Baroness set her hoof on the turf of the Curragh Racecourse for the first time. Consisting of six thousand sprawling acres, it was an endless windswept plain that stretched as far as she could see.

Tiffany stood her to the side of the conditioning track for a short while, allowing her time to get her bearings. More than anything, she wanted Baroness to feel relaxed. There was no sense in pressuring her too early because there would be pressure enough when she raced.

When the girl finally asked her for a slow trot, Baroness could feel the easy give and take of her fingers on the reins, delicately moving the bit in her mouth. As soon as Baroness would give in to it, Tiffany would lessen her hold ever so slightly, then take it up again until the filly's neck was rounded and she was properly on the bit.

"Good girl," Tiffany praised and ran her hand down her mane. She was trying to be reassuring to the filly, yet Baroness could still sense some hesitation on her part. After all, this was the first time she had been on a horse since she was hurt, and it was only natural that she would be wary.

The fresh air smelled of spring as Baroness inhaled the scent of green grass and newly tilled fields from the surrounding farms. She listened to the distant hoofbeats of a fleet of approaching horses, and as they came into view she saw that there were nine of them, all running along easily. The warm air from their nostrils formed clouds in front of them as they exhaled, and as they came nearer, Baroness could see steam rising off their sweaty bodies through the mist. She cocked one ear back to listen to Tiffany, who spoke hearteningly.

"You're doing fine," she said. "There's no need to fear these horses, they're just like you."

The thoroughbreds glided along in four pairs with one young straggler bringing up the rear. As they passed, Baroness fought her urge to run in the opposite direction, and she made herself stay quiet and wait for her friend's next instructions.

As the lone straggler galloped alongside them, Baroness felt the tap of the girl's heels to her sides, telling her it was time to go. Baroness' legs were so shaky that she almost stumbled with her first step. There was another rap of the heels, and she felt Tiffany's hands lower slightly, giving slack to the reins and allowing Baroness to take her head and move forward.

The filly took another step, then she took two more, and before she knew it, she was moving alongside the last horse at an uneven trot. Glancing over at it, Baroness realized that it was a young colt not much older than she. He was concentrating so hard on what his rider was asking him to do that he did not notice her at first.

"Good morning," she said with a little nicker.

The colt's eyes darted over to her, and he gave her a hurried nod just as the rider touched his hind quarters with a crop, telling him to pay attention. Baroness felt an instant regret that she had gotten him in trouble, and she fixed her eyes in front of her and continued her jog.

"This is not the place for socializing," she told herself. "I'll have to apologize to him later."

As they trotted up a slight incline, Baroness could tell from the way that the reins were trembling that Tiffany was lacking strength. It was so unsettling that a few times, when Baroness wanted to pull on the reins to move faster, she kept herself in check because she knew that this was as much a test for Tiffany as it was for her. When they reached the crest of the slope, she pulled slightly on the bit and Tiffany gave in, allowing her to go faster. Effortlessly extending her stride, she came alongside Jenny Mae, who looked over at her and smiled.

"Your lass is hanging onto you nicely," she commented, between breaths. "They say she's brave to be up in the saddle again."

Baroness' eyes took on an affectionate glow. "She makes me feel brave because of it. Brave riders make brave horses."

Tiffany's weight shifted back in the saddle, and there was a little tug on the bit which Baroness took to mean that she was going too fast. Slackening her gait, she felt Tiffany lightly touch her withers with one finger.

"Good girl," she said as she moved her to the inside of the track. When she was positioned correctly, she then tapped the horse on both sides of her neck with her reins. Baroness knew that she meant for her to stride out again, and when she did, Tiffany gave her the same positive feedback.

"I'll not use a whip on you," Tiffany told her as she allowed Baroness to gallop out the rest of the way. "You'll learn to run because you want to, not because I demand it."

Tiffany was shaking when they finally pulled up at the starting point. Sweat was streaming down her face and she looked very pale as she walked Baroness back to the barn and removed her saddle. From her fatigued appearance, the grey filly thought that the girl had worked the hardest of the two of them.

Removing her bridle, she put Baroness' halter back on her and proceeded to walk her down the lane and through the fields of sheep and cattle to the pond where they used to go. The sweat had dried on Baroness' coat, and her breathing was steady and relaxed compared to Tiffany's huffing breaths. As she dipped her snout into the cool water of the pond, Baroness heard Tiffany start to laugh.

Baroness turned to look at the girl, just as Tiffany wrapped her arms around the horse's neck. Laying the side of her face against it, she laughed harder and Baroness knew that this was a special moment.

"We did it!" Tiffany declared happily. "I don't think anyone really believed we would, except you and me."

Taking a strand of her carrot-colored hair between her lips, Baroness nibbled on it and Tiffany kissed her once on the neck.

The weeks of training passed happily for Baroness and Tiffany, and with each other to depend on, the confidence of both horse and rider steadily improved. Baroness won her first time out, and followed up the initial win with two successive victories. She had impressed the racing world with her natural ability, and by the end of her two-year-old campaign, she was considered one of the top fillies in thoroughbred racing. When it came time to race as a three-year-old, her talent was so glorious that she was invited to run in one of Ireland's most celebrated races for fillies, the Oaks.

Her stablemate was still Jenny Mae, and the two fillies would spend the early mornings together jogging across the green open area of the Curragh. They would often have exchanges about what the other horses were doing, and what was going on around the racecourse. Unfortunately though, most of the recent conversation centered around Savage. There was talk of how brilliantly he was training, but also about how he had tried to injure his lad almost every day. He was so unruly that he could no longer be galloped in company because he tried to harm horses as well.

"They say he is absolutely crazy," Jenny Mae told Baroness as they trotted alongside each other. "I heard that he holds a grudge forever, and if he doesn't like you, he'll not just try to hurt you, he'll try to kill you. He especially hates Tiffany because she is the one that broke him, and that is why he flipped her. He told the colt in the stall next to his that he watches her go by every morning and he's just waiting for the chance to get to her."

They passed a thicket of trees, and two small bunnies darted in front of them. Baroness swerved without being asked, she never tripped when she was at a jog or a canter. Her big feet only got in the way when she tried to walk.

"I wouldn't let that happen to Tiffany ever," Baroness responded seriously. "Anyway, I think he's just crazy and doesn't really know what he is saying. Some horses are like that. It wouldn't matter if they were racing or turned out in a pasture to do as they pleased, they would still be miserable."

Jenny Mae looked off into the distance without a reply, then her rider tapped her on the hindquarters with the whip, asking her to go faster.

"Give me more, Baroness," the filly heard Tiffany urge, and in a moment, the two fillies were neck-in-neck running against each other.

Because Baroness' stride was considerably longer than Jenny Mae's, she kept up easily, and when she felt Tiffany give her the bit and ask her again, Baroness gathered her strength and shot ahead of Jenny Mae with incredible speed.

"Give me more, Baroness!" she heard her rider ask again, and soon she was digging in and going faster just with the urging of Tiffany's voice.

She headed up a grassy incline feeling thoroughly in command of herself, knowing that she could go even faster if she was asked. For the first time ever, she allowed her mind to fill with the fantasy of racing in the Oaks. She imagined that at that very moment, she was running down the homestretch toward the finish line, and there was not a horse in the field who could catch her. She even entertained the idea that her performance was so astounding that news of her victory would travel across the ocean to the farm in America where she was born, and the mother and father she had never known would hear of her accomplishment.

She imagined that the prize money was enough to replace Tiffany's inheritance, and that would be Baroness' way of repaying her for believing in her all this time.

Baroness was so caught up in the thought of this that she did not notice that a strange horse had bolted behind her. All she had seen was a dark flash. She passed yet another horse before she heard the thud of hooves running up on her, and all at once she realized that the brown blur of a horse was now at her shoulder. She could hear its heavy breathing and the menacing grunts he let out with every other stride. Feeling Tiffany jolt in the saddle, she looked out of the corner of her eye and saw its massive head turn and show its teeth as it tried to bite her.

The rider on the brown horse yelled something, and Baroness felt Tiffany stiffen with fear and grab hold of Baroness' mane with both hands. To the young filly, that was a signal that Tiffany had placed all of her trust in her, and that whoever it was that was running alongside them was someone to fear.

"Give me more, Baroness," Tiffany cried. "Please, give me more!"

Stretching out her neck, Baroness reached inside herself and found more speed, pulling ahead of her pursuer. She was approaching the stable area, but did not want to stop because the chase was still on. She could clearly see the dark streak coming up on her again. Its rider was shouting for him to halt and was pulling so hard on his reins that the horse's mouth was cut and bleeding, but still it did not give up.

Turning to the right, Baroness headed down a gravel drive and bolted across the two-lane road to the open country on the other side. She heard the honking of car horns, and the screeching of brakes behind her as she leaped off the pavement and onto soft footing, continuing her run.

There was a mass of confusion, and people were yelling that the horses were loose. Everyone seemed to be screaming but Tiffany, who just held on tightly to Baroness' mane. Then someone shouted a single word and it made Baroness' blood run cold. They only had to utter it once for Baroness to realize that the brown blur she was struggling to outrun was Savage.

She did not know how it happened, if she had simply stopped or if in all the confusion Savage had dashed around her right flank and stood her off. But the next thing she knew, he was standing directly in front of her, his eyes blazing with fury and daring her to challenge him. He was now riderless, and blood from the sides of his cut mouth mixed with his angry froth and dripped from his lips. His bridle was broken, and the snaffle bit was dangling loosely beneath his chin.

Baroness had never seen such a terrible sight in her life. She stood perfectly still, fully aware that Tiffany was relying on her completely. If Savage attacked, he would attack them both, and because Tiffany never used a whip when she rode her, the girl would be defenseless.

There was a stand of trees located a few yards behind where Savage was standing. Baroness reasoned that if she could get past the angry mass of horseflesh pacing in front of her, they might offer some protection.

Lowering her head submissively, she first tried to show the furious colt that she was not challenging him. She did not dare make a sound. By the way he was snorting and pawing the ground, she knew that any attempt to speak with him would only anger him more. Then it occurred to her that if he truly was as crazy as they said, he might just let them go by if Baroness showed no fear.

A chilling silence suddenly surrounded them as if all that existed was the two thoroughbreds and the girl, whom Baroness was determined to protect. Looking upward, she met Savage's eye, wordlessly telling him that she wanted no violence. He flaunted his thick black tail behind him, and took in a huge breath that seemed to make his taut muscles swell so big that they looked like they would burst through his skin. The morning sun caught the pupil of his sharp eye, making it flare, and his ears were pinned back as he took a step forward.

Still, Baroness did not move. She thought he was using his cunning to test her courage. She believed that if she did not waver, surely someone would come to rescue them from this brute.

She felt Tiffany's hands tighten on her mane as she crouched low and forward at the same moment that Savage made a headlong rush into her. Baroness felt the force of his body shove her backward, but rather than give up her ground, she rose up on her two hind legs and attempted to stave him off by jabbing at him with her front hooves. She could hear his jaws clamping shut on the air in front of her as he tried to grab hold of her forelegs, and Tiffany cried out and started tugging at the reins to try to hold her back. Then Savage retreated a few steps before he too reared up and came at her, the steel on his hooves powerfully flashing in the sunlight.

Baroness was fearless as she struck back at him, hitting him in the snout as she screamed a shrill cry of warning that he should not to come any closer. She felt a wrath rising in her, but it was not to do harm, rather it was to do what she must to keep Tiffany safe. Whirling around, she was able to kick him in the left flank with her back legs and knock him off balance. As she did this, she caught sight of the stable-hands approaching with whips and ropes, but she knew they would not reach them in time.

Suddenly, there was the scrambling of hooves, and when Baroness turned to face him again, he was looming over her, sucking violent breaths into his lungs and screaming louder than she had ever heard a horse scream before. Tiffany was screaming too, screaming for someone to help them and for Savage to stop, but he paid no heed.

It seemed an eternity before he pinned his ears back again, bared his teeth, and made one more vicious attack on them. Baroness could feel the impact of his hooves and the stinging pain as he struck her in the face and neck, trying to get at Tiffany.

Raising one foreleg to defend herself, Baroness saw a spurt of crimson as he wrenched it between his teeth in a fit of utter rage. In the next moment, the stablehands were on him and beating him back. It took four of them, all wielding crops or leather lead ropes, before he finally released Baroness' leg.

Staggering to the side, the grey filly turned on her heels and in a flash, she was running toward home. She could hear Tiffany weeping and slurring together words she could not understand. The girl was so frightened that all Baroness could think of to do was to get them home again. When she turned down the lane to their stables, she was glad to see Tiffany's father running toward them.

He grabbed the reins and pulled Baroness to a halt, then helped Tiffany from the saddle. The filly could feel her muscles twitching nervously as she kept looking behind her to be sure Savage had not followed. She was trotting in place, skittishly moving from side to side. She knew she had been hurt by his blows, but her body was still too numb with fear for her to feel very much pain. Running her hand down her foreleg, Tiffany lifted it, saw the blood, and cried even harder.

"There, there, Tiffany," her father tried to comfort her. "He bit her just below the knee. Let's wait for the vet to examine her. Hopefully, there won't be too much damage."

Tiffany took Baroness' head in her arms and kissed her on the forehead. "I'm sorry this happened to you," she wept. "But thank you for protecting me."

Baroness lowered her head, then jerked it back up and looked over her shoulder again to be certain that Savage was no longer there.

CHAPTER TWELVE-A

An Uncertain Future

"SHE'S GOING TO BE very sore. There's been some damage to her leg, but I'm not sure how much it will affect her running. We'll just have to see how she heals," the veterinarian told Tiffany and her father as he finished putting the last of the stitches into Baroness' foreleg.

The courageous filly stood with only Tiffany holding onto her. She was trying her best to keep still because she did not want to upset the girl more than she already was.

"You're so brave," Tiffany told her, her voice cracking with emotion. "You're so very brave, Baroness."

"Certainly, she was," the vet agreed. "The horse she fought with is missing his two front teeth. I almost expected to find them stuck in her foreleg."

Both Tiffany and her father started to laugh, but as soon as the smile broadened on Tiffany's face, she began to cry again.

"Will she be all right?" she asked, wiping her tears away with the back of her hand. It was as if she had been afraid to pose the question for fear of what the answer might be.

"I think she's going to be fine. There will be some swelling and she'll need rest, but time heals everything."

"Unfortunately, time is the one thing we don't have a lot of," Mr. O'Connell interjected. He lowered his head and slowly walked over to a feed bucket, and turning it upside down, used it as a seat. "We were pointing her toward the Oaks next month. Is there a chance she could make it?"

The veterinarian snipped the thread of the last stitch and looked the filly up and down skeptically.

"I don't see how," he answered. "It's not that she won't be healed, but the conditioning she'll loose during her recovery will be enough to count her out. That is a very tough race, and she would have to be at her peak performance. I'd look for another race if I were you."

"It'll be too late by then," Mr. O'Connell said dejectedly. "I was counting on a good showing to pay off a debt. If I don't have the money, they'll take Baroness as payment."

Baroness grumbled as Tiffany's jaw dropped open in astonishment.

"What do you mean, Father?" she asked.

Resting his elbows on his knees, Mr. O'Connell stared down at the ground. His brow had deep furrows in it and when he looked up at his daughter, his eyes were clouded with remorse.

"I made some bets that did not work out, Tiffany," he said shamefully. "They were horses that I thought were certain to pay nicely, but they did not come in the way I expected. Baroness was doing so well that I borrowed money against what she was worth. If I don't have it to pay back by next month, we'll have to sign her over to the bookmakers and they'll race her themselves."

Tiffany looked at her father in disbelief. He had never been a gambler, and to borrow money from anyone—least of all the bookmakers—was entirely out of his character. He had always been the one who advised her never to give them information on the horses she rode and never to accept their bribes. "You had no right to do that. I bought this filly with the money my mother left to me."

There was a long silence, and Baroness looked at Tiffany, then at her father, waiting for one of them to speak. She could see how awful they both felt, and it made her sad because she knew that father and daughter cared for each other deeply. Then Tiffany turned her attention to the vet. "How soon can she start jogging?"

"As soon as all the swelling goes down," he answered.

"If I give her a few days rest, can I start hand-walking her?" she asked.

"Yes, you can. We'll need to keep a close eye on her to be sure that the wounds on her legs don't fill up with fluid. I'll work as closely with you as I can, Tiffany, but some things are going to have to depend on her. If she can work through the pain, it will be in her favor."

Tiffany looked Baroness directly in the eye. "I know she'll do her best," she said loud enough for only the filly to hear.

That night, Tiffany fell asleep in Baroness' stall. She had spent the better part of the night weeping and apologizing to the horse for endangering her. Baroness could scarcely understand why; no one could be blamed for what had happened, not even Savage. Perhaps he was not as crazy as he was unhappy, Baroness thought. Perhaps what he wanted more than to race was to remain free and untamed like his ancestors before him, and maybe he did not hate men as much as he despised what they did to him by climbing on his back and making him obey. Not every horse could read the face of a human and tell by its expression whether it was appreciated or not.

Then there was Tiffany. Poor, poor, Tiffany, Baroness thought, as she recalled the way the girl had cried for hours. She seemed more upset about what had taken place than Baroness. Now she sat exhausted and huddled in the corner beneath the feed tub with her legs drawn up to her chest and her face hidden behind her bent knees.

The filly stood over her protectively for a long time, wondering what would have become of her if Tiffany had not cared so much. She had seen it in the girl's face that day at the auction. It was the look of gentle understanding, a look that Savage had probably never recognized. Still, Baroness knew that she would never be able to forget the burning in his eyes. They had looked like hot coals, and behind them lurked an angry being that was ready to lash out at anything that stood in his way. Shaking herself to get rid of the image, Baroness felt the ache in her body from the blows he had inflicted, yet it seemed trivial compared to the sadness that Tiffany must have felt when she heard of her father's gambling.

Limping closer to the girl, she sniffed her hair, then expanded her nostrils and took in her human scent. She found it strange how the two of them could have been made so differently and still have so much in common. Tiffany had never known her mother, nor had Baroness. Tiffany walked on two legs and Baroness walked on four. Yet when she carried the girl on her back, she had the feeling that they were one being and that there was nothing that could ever separate them.

She watched her for a long time, but the girl did not stir, so Baroness ambled over to the stall door and stuck out her head. In a moment, Jenny Mae's head popped out as well.

"They said you're going to be all right, Baroness," Jenny Mae said. "I heard that Savage wanted to hurt you and Tiffany, but you didn't let him."

Baroness shrugged. "To tell you the truth, Jenny Mae, I don't really know what I did. I just didn't want him to get Tiffany again."

Jenny Mae nodded. "You sure were running fast, I couldn't believe it myself. One minute you were next to me, then you were gone across the road. It's a shame that you had to tangle with him though. This is the worst thing he's ever done to anybody."

"It's a strange thing with him because I honestly don't think he knows what he is doing," Baroness replied. "Looking back on it, I don't think he has any idea of right and wrong. I think he just wants to hurt others because he feels hurt himself. Maybe he doesn't like racing and that's why he's so mean."

Jenny Mae raised her brows. "I never thought about that. He's just such a menace that I thought you would hate him, not be sympathetic toward him."

The filly took a nibble from her hay bag. "I'm not sure what I feel about him, I only know that I'm never going to let myself be afraid of him. I'll never try to fight him, but I'll never cower from him either."

Jenny Mae craned her neck forward and tried to peek into Baroness' stall. "Did she stop crying?" she asked, referring to Tiffany.

Baroness nodded. "She cried herself to sleep. She's worried that I'll not make the Oaks, and that she'll have to sign me over to the bookmakers because of her father's debts."

Jenny Mae's eyes started to tear. "I'd hate to see you go away. I know that Mr. O'Connell placed some bets because they were short of money when Tiffany was sick and couldn't work. It surprised me when I heard it because I know that he is normally not a gambling man. I heard that he was counting on you to win so that he could pay back what he owes. Whatever happens after this, I don't think he'll ever try that again."

Baroness started to answer, but was distracted by a muscle spasm moving up her leg to her shoulder. Looking at it, she could see the tiny twitches around the area where Savage had struck, then she looked down at her bandaged foreleg.

"Well, Jenny Mae," she said, her voice clear and determined. "I hope he hasn't given up on me yet."

Three days passed before Baroness was able to walk without any pain. She was dutifully attended to by Tiffany, who spent every spare minute with the filly, trying to keep her spirits up. She fed her carrots and sugar cubes and even sang to her in the evening while she ate. Baroness loved the sound of her melodic voice because it had a beautiful pitch to it that was as unique to the Irish people as their natural talent for handling horses. However, although Baroness' physical condition improved, she became more emotionally distressed at the relationship that had developed between Tiffany and her father.

It was plain that Mr. O'Connell felt terrible about the situation, and Tiffany did too, but the two dealt with it by ignoring each other most of the time. When they did speak, they were very impatient and curt.

On the morning of the fourth day, Tiffany arrived early to feed and groom Baroness. When she was finished, she put the filly's halter on her, and took her out of the stall. It was overcast, but Baroness was glad to be out just the same. They walked down the lane and stopped at the sheep field. Tiffany looked carefully at Baroness' bandages and felt around the collar of her neck to be sure she was not getting overheated. Then they proceeded to enter the field. A few of the sheep called out to them, and Baroness whinnied back. One little lamb even came right up to her with a smile and tried to make friends.

Baroness stopped and looked at it. It was small and fluffy and as she dropped her head to sniff it, it stuck its little black nose right into her snout.

"You're so tall," it said.

"Yes, I am tall," Baroness replied, still standing nose to nose with the lamb.

"Do you like being that big?" it asked with curiousity.

"Sometimes yes and sometimes no," she answered. "But that's just the way I was made, and I can't do too much about it."

"Oh well, I guess you're right about that. My name is Buster," the lamb introduced himself.

"Pleased to meet you, Buster. My name is Baroness."

"Baroness, huh. You're not from around here, I can tell by your accent."

"No, I was born in America," she answered. "I was brought here two summers ago."

Buster took a mouthful of grass. "You ever think about going back?" he asked.

"No, not really. My home is here now, and this is where I race."

The lamb filled his mouth with more grass and glanced over at Tiffany. "You think she knows what we're talking about?"

The grey filly shrugged. "Maybe not word for word, but I think she understands that we're saying hello."

Tiffany gave a gentle tug on the Baroness' lead, and as she continued walking, Buster followed.

"You mind if I tag along? I've never had the chance to talk to a horse before."

"I don't mind at all, but won't your mother miss you?"

"Not if I don't go too far," he replied, but a moment later, the baa of his mother could be heard calling him to come back.

Buster ignored her and hopped along beside Baroness. It took all his effort to keep up with her because he was so small.

"Don't you think you should go back? She's calling you." Baroness asked, concerned. "I wouldn't want you to get in trouble."

The lamb looked over his fluffy shoulder, then turned his attention in front of him once more. "If she really wants me, she'll come after me. She's not real crazy about people, so maybe your friend might keep her away. My mother doesn't like the way people always say that we sheep are stupid."

"Well, if someone called me stupid, I wouldn't like it either," Baroness commented. "They usually don't call racehorses stupid—not if they win."

Buster shrugged. "I don't let it get to me because they don't realize that they could not do what we do. I don't know a single human who could eat grass all day and turn it into wool. We don't hurt anybody, and we grow clothes for people right on our back. Not only that, but we all live here in peace, and we hardly ever have a disagreement with each other. That doesn't seem stupid to me."

The lamb stopped talking because the three of them were at the pond by this time.

"Say, what happened to you anyway?" he asked as Baroness dipped her mouth into the water to have a drink.

"You mean my leg? I got into a tangle with another horse," she replied licking her lips. "I didn't start it though because I really hate to fight."

Buster stared at his reflection in the glassy surface of the pond as she answered him, then touched his velvety black nose to it. The ripples of the water caused both his and Baroness' images to bend. Baroness whinnied at the sight of it, and Buster baaed with delight. Then, they heard the long, whining bleat of another sheep as his mother appeared in the grass behind him. Her expression was stern, and she was shaking her head.

"Buster, I told you not to wander so far! Come back to the fold!" she commanded.

Buster looked up at Baroness and gave a tedious sigh. "I better be on my way now. Maybe I'll see you again sometime. Try to stay out of fights, all right?"

"All right. Good-bye Buster," she said.

Baroness stared after him as he moved toward his mother with a series of short leaps, then she heard him baa once more as the sheep gave him a tiny nip on the back of the neck to show her displeasure.

Turning back to Tiffany, Baroness noticed that she had a troubled look about her as she stared down at her own reflection. The water on the pond became still once again, and the filly rested her chin on the girl's shoulder to comfort her.

CHAPTER FOURTEEN

Training at Laytown

"I WANT YOU TO KNOW that I am entirely against this!" Mr. O'Connell loudly declared.

He was standing in the shedrow just outside of the stall, watching Tiffany put on Baroness' traveling bandages. The trailer was waiting behind him, ready to take the girl and her filly to Laytown, a small seaside resort on the east coast of Ireland.

Tiffany finished applying the standing wrap she was working on, then reached for another and started bandaging Baroness' back legs. They were headed for the beach, where Baroness could train for the big race in the saltwater and soft sand.

As Tiffany exited the stall, Baroness stuck her head out and she and Jenny Mae watched the exchange between the father and daughter. Both wore very austere expressions as they grumbled a few words to each other, then Tiffany loaded her suitcase and tack trunk into the van and addressed Mr. O'Connell with her arms folded stubbornly across her chest.

"The vet said that the left front tendon is worse than he

originally thought, and shouldn't be stressed any more than is needed," she said. Her tone was not angry, just very matter-of-fact. "She might only have one race in her, and I want her to have the best chance of winning, that's why I want to gallop her on the beach. Besides, the saltwater will be good for her legs. I'm not running away from home like you might think. I just want to train my filly the best way I know how. It might not be what you would do with your horse, Father, but please try to trust my judgement. I know what is best for her. You know that I would never disobey you, so I'm asking you, please, give me your permission so I can leave with a clear conscience."

Mr. O'Connell put his hand to his brow, then dropped it and looked at his daughter with an apologetic expression. "I'll worry about you both," he said softly. "Tiffany, I'm so sorry about all of this."

Tears welled in Tiffany's eyes. "I know you are. I'm sure you didn't mean any harm, you only did what you had to do. Now I'm doing what I have to do. I've already told Granny that Baroness and I are coming."

A tear trickled down her cheek as she went forward and placed her arms around her father's neck. He hugged her close for a minute, then released her and forced a smile.

"You'd make your mother proud, and surely your granny will be happy to see you," he said. "Well then, I'll see you the night before the race."

"We'll be there," she answered, smiling back at him. "You just take care of the jockey who is going to ride her. If it is a different one than she is used to, tell him ahead of time that he can't use a whip on her. She won't run for anyone who would hit her. Make that very clear."

Baroness turned to Jenny Mae with a happy expression. "I think things are getting better already."

Jenny Mae whinnied her approval. "They sure are. Now if you just do your part, everything will be better still. You know Baroness, if you win this race, you'll be famous."

"I don't care about that, Jenny Mae," she responded sincerely. "I just want a chance to repay some of the kindness that Tiffany has shown me. Why, if she hadn't been there for me, who knows where I would have ended up."

"Well, when you're a big star, will you still want to gallop with me in the morning?" Jenny Mae asked shyly.

Baroness gave her friend a kind smile. She knew that it must have been hard on Jenny Mae when visitors always paid more attention to Baroness than to her, and sometimes she felt left out. "Jenny Mae, you're my friend. I wouldn't give up our friendship just because I won a race."

Jenny Mae nodded. "I know that, Baroness. I was silly to even think it. I'll miss you until you come back."

"Me too," Baroness agreed as Tiffany led her out of the stall and onto the trailer. "See you in a few weeks, Jenny Mae."

Slowly traveling the winding roads past Dublin to the coast, Baroness watched out the window as flowery meadows and pastoral fields went by. She knew when she was getting close to the sea because the smell of the air became salty and musty, and the land turned from sloping hillsides to a more rocky terrain. After pulling up a dirt road, the van stopped, and Tiffany opened the trailer doors and unloaded her.

Baroness stepped off the trailer with her ears straight up and her nostrils wide with the smell of the ocean. The weather was a bit foggy, so Tiffany immediately put a blanket on her so she would not get a chill. They walked down a narrow path past a stone cottage to a two-stall barn. It was already bedded with fresh straw, and as soon as Baroness was turned loose, she rolled in it to scratch her back.

Tiffany went over to the back door of the cottage and knocked. The door was opened by an elderly woman who greeted her with a warm hug, then invited her indoors. In a moment, the engine hum of the transport van sounded, and it went on its way back toward Dublin.

Baroness stared after it for a few minutes, and her stomach started to quiver at being all alone in a strange place. Then she gazed into the distance at the rhythmic tide rolling in from the sea. This was such an isolated place, she thought, not one where she would ever want to be by herself. However, she did not have to worry because as long as Tiffany was with her, she knew she would feel at home.

At nightfall, Tiffany rolled out her sleeping bag in the empty stall beside Baroness. The straw was clean but damp from the mist blowing in off the water, and as the filly lay down, her ears filled with the girl's shallow breaths, and soon she fell fast asleep.

It was almost noon the next day when Baroness and Tiffany descended the trail to the beach. The shore was deserted, and except for the rolling sound of the water as it moved up and back on the sand, it was completely silent as well. It was a long, lonely strand with an empty field overlooking it. There was a racecourse there when the tide was out, but on this day it was completely covered by water.

The girl and the thoroughbred walked along the tide's edge, and every so often the salty, foaming liquid would rise up around Baroness' ankles, then fall back again. Although the wounds from Savage's teeth were healing well, her left leg was still very weak where he had gripped it in his teeth.

When Tiffany walked her up to the dry sand, Baroness thought it very strange that she removed her saddle, as well as her own riding clothes, revealing a bright yellow swim suit. Then she took hold of the reins and led the horse into the water. As it rose up around her knees, Baroness instinctively pulled back, but Tiffany firmly held onto her.

"You're all right," she told her as she gently tugged on the reins and urged Baroness another step forward.

The water was now above Tiffany's knees, and Baroness stopped short. Lifting her foreleg, she began pawing at it and causing it to splash up in her face. She let out a concerned neigh that was meant to tell Tiffany that she did not want to go any farther, but Tiffany just laughed good-naturedly.

"I said you're all right," she repeated. "Come out just a little farther. I promise I won't let anything happen to you."

With the next step Baroness felt the ground break away beneath her. Panicked, she started trying to run but found that the clop of her hooves only created noisy splashes in the ocean around her. Sticking her nose up in the air, she neighed again, and as the saltwater dripped off her nose and into her open mouth, she felt the familiar weight of Tiffany on her back.

"Just relax, Baroness," she soothed, running her hand down her mane. "We're going for a swim."

Soon Baroness found herself moving along effortlessly as the sparkling sea rose up around her body. It felt like it was supporting her entirely. Trusting Tiffany's judgement, she soon forgot about her fear and found herself actually enjoying it.

When she took her first few steps back out onto the sand, it felt very odd because she had briefly become accustomed to the weightlessness. Shaking herself, she then trotted a few steps, but pulled up short because her leg felt very tight. Slowing her to a walk, Tiffany waded her back into the water and allowed her to stand in it for a long time while it pooled around her knees.

The weeks passed rapidly as Baroness' training regimen increased. She would walk farther up the beach each day, then swim for awhile before jogging back at a comfortable pace.

With every setting sun, Tiffany would faithfully check the condition her leg, then wrap it in a clay poultice so it would not swell. Were it not for this invisible injury, Baroness would have appeared to be made of steel. Her big, rangy build rippled with each step, and the muscles in her hindquarters were so defined that they made shadowy crevices in the sunlight. Only the tendon offered any reason to doubt that she would win any race that she entered.

On the last afternoon before they were due to return to the Curragh, Tiffany and Baroness spent a rare sunny day picnicking on the beach. The sand was very warm, and as soon as Tiffany unclasped the shank from her halter, Baroness lowered herself and rolled in it. She loved the feel of it as it slid down her coat and the way it sprayed like water in all directions when she shook. Tiffany had brought the filly's hay bag and set it out for her to munch on while she ate her own lunch.

The girl seemed very serious as she stared out at the horizon for a long while, then she looked solemnly at Baroness.

She had tears in her eyes, and when she started to speak, her lips trembled.

"I don't even want to think that anyone could take you away from me," she told the filly in a shaky voice.

Baroness raised her head and sighed then went back to her hay. She kept one ear cocked in Tiffany's direction, attentively listening to everything she was saying.

"I don't even know if I should ask you to run in the race," she went on. "You serve me so well that if something were to happen to you, I'd never forgive myself. If the bookmakers were to take you and race you themselves, I know you would break down for sure, and I can't let that happen."

Extending her hand, she ran her palm down the horse's left foreleg. The tendon was tight and cool and showed no signs of swelling, but it had yet to be tested against the rigorous pounding of a race.

"I've never asked a horse not to try," she murmured, dropping her head. "And I've never met a horse who wouldn't try if asked. All I can do is tell your jockey that if your leg starts to go, he should pull up on you straightaway. Not even a bookmaker would want a horse who can't race again, because there's no money in that. It's different for me; I'd take you in any condition. You and I will be friends forever."

CHAPTER FIFTEEN

The Final Challenge

ON THE MORNING of the race, Tiffany took Baroness out for a light jog before going back to the track stable. All of the entrants for the Oaks were stabled in one barn. It was made of slate grey stucco and located in a central square with patches of worn grass and no trees at all.

Tiffany meticulously groomed her filly because in addition to it being a matter of personal pride that Baroness looked her best, there was also prize of one hundred pounds awarded to the best turned out horse, and she wanted to win it.

Brushing Baroness' grey coat to a luster, she then unbraided the horse's mane, which had been plaited the night before so when it was brushed out, it fell in loose black curls down her neck. Her whiskers, ears, and the area just behind her forelock—called the bridle path—were shaved closely, and so was the fur along her pasterns.

All of the fillies running that day were filled with a sense of great anticipation. The Oaks was the fillies' version of the Irish Derby, and in a country like Ireland, which is known for

its tremendous thoroughbreds, to win such a celebrated title meant being considered amongst its best.

Yet for Baroness, it meant even more than that because she knew that if she did not make a good showing, she and Tiffany would be separated forever, and the thought of it was more than she could take. Tiffany was the one who had befriended her and showed her that she was as good as any other thoroughbred, and all of bravery and special attention she bestowed on Baroness made her believe in herself all the more.

Although the eager filly did not fully understand the importance of the money that was owed by Mr. O'Connell, or even how much Tiffany had spent to buy her, all she knew was that the mysterious printed paper greatly affected the most important person in her life, and she wanted desperately not to let her down.

After giving Baroness her grain, Tiffany left for a short time. When she returned, her carrot-colored hair was pulled back in a braid, and she was dressed in a white linen shirt that buttoned down the front. She had on pleated riding trousers, and her paddock boots were newly shined.

Using an overturned feedbucket as a stool, she sat just outside of Baroness' stall humming a soft, sweet melody to the horse to keep her relaxed. Baroness knew when the race was drawing near because Tiffany brushed the dust from her coat once more, picked out her hooves, and put race wraps on her forelegs. These were thin, woven elastic bandages that started just below the knee and extended down the cannon bone, covering the fetlock joint. They felt much tighter than the bandages that Baroness wore in the morning when she jogged, but she liked the feel of the extra support they gave her tendons.

Baroness looked at Tiffany expectantly as the girl stood back, and happily took in the filly's appearance. Then her eyes rested on the left foreleg and her expression became very grim. Baroness wished she could tell her that it did not hurt, and she would run as fast as she could for as long as it would carry her. But all she could do was trustingly press her brow into the girl's shoulder.

"Calling the horses for the next race," a man's gravelly voice was heard from the gate, causing Baroness to straighten and paw the ground in front of her.

She was ready to go — ready to run even faster than on the day Savage had chased her. Only this time she would not run out of fear; she would run out of confidence. She knew that with enough desire and a little race luck, she could bring in a win for herself and her lass.

As she stepped out into the afternoon sunlight, she caught sight of her shadow. Because of the time of day, it was very small compared to her actual size, and for a brief instant she recalled her earliest memory of being walked past a majestic chestnut stallion on her way to the pasture. She remembered how he had stared at her so kindly, as though he wanted to say something special to her. And it was so touching the way the grey mare stood behind him, her head lowered to hide the empty sockets where her eyes should have been.

"Is that her, Freddie?" she had quietly asked him. "Is she all right?"

"She's fine. She will be grey, just like you, Rosie," was all he said to her, and Baroness recalled having the feeling that he kept his eye on her long after she had gone by.

"I will be fine," she told herself and whinnied.

Baroness started dancing in place when she first saw the wide, green plain of the Curragh racecourse. Even though she had jogged on it earlier that morning, on race days it was as exciting as seeing it for the very first time. The air was restless with spectators, and their murmurings drifted on the breeze to Baroness' ears, adding to her delight. She liked the brightly colored finery worn by the wealthy women and the bowler hats sported by the gentry. But when she strutted past the bookmakers, each had a swarm of bettors shoving banknotes into their hands. She let out a scream of defiance as though she were just taunting them to bet against her.

"Easy, Baroness," Tiffany coaxed. "There's no need to make this personal."

Baroness was chomping at the bit, and by the time she and Tiffany entered the paddock, she was prancing and throwing her head. They kept walking around the circular area and she took in the spectators looking at the sheets of betting predictions and shrewdly sizing up the field of fillies to run. Then there came the official judgment on which of the horses was groomed the best, and Baroness could feel Tiffany's hand tighten around the shank as it was announced.

"The stewards have finally come to an agreement for the best turned out filly for the the Oaks," a voice boomed over the loudspeaker. "An award of one hundred pounds will be given to the groom of Baroness."

Tiffany gave Baroness a small kiss on the tip of her nose. "You would be beautiful no matter who groomed you," she whispered to her.

They followed the rest of the horses out onto the track to be paraded in front of the crowd. By this time, Baroness was so excited that she could barely be contained. She kept walking in front of Tiffany, and the girl was using all her strength to hang onto her.

When it came time to jog in front of the grandstand, Baroness was raising and lowering her legs like a carousel horse, and the sound of the muffled approval from the crowd only added to her anticipation. No longer was she the awkward horse whose feet were too big, who ran not because she loved it, but because she was always afraid. She knew now that courage and confidence came from being loved for who she was. With that and her lineage, she had every reason to expect excellence from herself.

The jockeys were on the grass now, and Baroness was halted regally in front of Mr. O'Connell and her rider, who had come over from England especially for this race.

"May I have your whip?" Tiffany asked him politely.

The jockey looked at her questioningly.

"She won't run if you hit her," the girl explained. "She has never been hit by anyone. All you need to do when you want her to run is say, 'Give me more, Baroness!' and she will."

"I've never heard of such a thing," the jockey remarked. "What if I ask, and she doesn't want to give me more?"

"She does, and she will. I would like your whip because I would hate it if, in a flustered moment, you forgot yourself and used it."

With one brow raised, the rider looked Baroness up and down skeptically. "Anything else?" he questioned, handing over his whip.

"Yes," Mr. O'Connell broke in. "Her left front leg is suspect, and we don't want to stress it needlessly. Keep her at a slow pace behind the others. She might only have one run in her, so gauge yourself. When you ask her to run, it better be for the finish. This filly is a battler, and because of her size, she can make up the distance as long as her leg holds out."

The jockey nodded, and Mr. O'Connell boosted him into the saddle.

"Remember, keep her off the pace and choose your move. She'll roll along just fine if you let her take the bit," he repeated.

Realizing this could be the last time they did this together, Tiffany gave her filly one last pat on the neck, but Baroness' mind was already on the race. With her ears pricked straight up, her large brown eyes were fixed on the open plain of the Curragh. She did not care who her competition was, nor did it matter who was riding her. All that was important was the few minutes ahead because in that brief span of time, her fate would be decided.

Moving at a brisk canter, Baroness took her place with the others and headed toward the starting gate. She did not look to the right or left of her, rather she kept her eyes downcast and tried to acquaint herself with the gestures of her rider. He had never ridden her before, yet his hands were soft, only moving the bit in her mouth when he wanted her to turn or slow her pace. Otherwise, they remained very still along the sides of her neck, and when they reached the start, he sat back in the saddle and stroked her mane.

Baroness was the first one in. She stood obediently, fighting her twitching muscles and her instinctive urge to bolt forward, as one by one the rest of the field was loaded into position. This was the hardest time of all she thought, because as much as she wanted to keep her mind on the race at hand, it kept drifting to Tiffany with the hopes that when this race was finished, she would be reunited with the girl who always made her feel so special.

As she heard the last gate slam shut, Baroness remembered once again the way the handsome chestnut stallion had gazed upon her from his paddock just days after her birth. She had no idea then that he had won so many races or that she would be in his first crop of runners. However, she knew all too well that if she won today, her performance would be a testimony to the greatness of their line.

"It is my right," she told herself. "I've earned the right to be great, as great as my sire was and as great a champion as his sire before him."

In the next instant, the gates burst open and Baroness broke a half a stride ahead of the others. Grass was flying behind them as the rumble of a mass of thoroughbred hooves filled the air like a bantering of drums. Without urging from her rider, she took her position at the rail. The field was close, so although she was first, the next runner was less than a half a length behind her, and before she knew it, a horse came from the outside to take away her lead.

The pace was fast, too fast for Baroness to maintain at such a long distance without harming her leg. She felt her rider pull back slightly, and when she did not respond, he tugged on her harder, and soon she found herself fighting against his hold.

Her nose was in the air, and she was jerking at the bit when she realized that in a split second, the field of horses had swallowed her up completely. She panicked.

"I have to run my hardest. I must win this race," she told herself as she watched the tails of the front runners streak farther and farther ahead of her.

The muscles in her entire body were bulging with energy, and the blood in her veins felt like a burning fire inside of her.

"They are going to beat me," she thought to herself. "If I don't make a run soon, I'll never be able to catch them."

Coming down the backstretch, the pace of the front runner started to fade, giving the impression that the rest of the fillies were quickening their gait. Yet, they stayed in a very close pack at least ten lengths in front of Baroness, who had now settled into a steady gallop under her jockey's command.

The field of runners continued along without changing positions, and as Baroness watched the first horse drop back into third place, she realized that not a single filly was challenging for the lead. They were all waiting for the perfect moment to make their final move, and Baroness feared that if one of them was game, she would not have the slightest chance of catching her.

All at once, it appeared that the runners slowed down. Either that or she had increased her speed without knowing it. She could not be sure. She only knew that she suddenly found herself gaining on the group of thoroughbreds, passing one horse on the outside, and darting between two more fillies to position herself in the middle of the pack. The sound of the crowd could only faintly be heard, yet the grandstand was now in sight which meant that it was time to think about the finish.

Baroness felt smooth and eager as she turned onto the homestretch. She asked her jockey to let her roll, and when at last, she felt the his stubborn hands start to yield, she knew she could make her final run.

Threading the needle between two more horses, she surged forward like a freight train. Her neck was stretched out and it appeared as though she was using her grey nose like a pointer, looking for the spaces of light between her competition that might allow to her tunnel through. She was quiet, yet determined as her jockey directed her perilously close to the rail. The space was so small that her big body brushed against it, yet she remained one accelerating shadow, bending and shaping herself until only a single horse remained in front of her.

The crowd was cheering her name as she inched to the lead. It was so loud that she barely heard it when her rider finally spoke.

"Give me more, Baroness!" he yelled, and jostled his reins. "Baroness, give me more!"

With her sleek legs reaching far out in front of her, Baroness took command of first place, then she suddenly swayed. Her left foreleg was faltering and she had scarcely created enough of a lead to canter out the rest of the race and still win. She had to find more.

Her jockey signalled for her to change leads but she could not do it, then he too, realized what was happening. He started to pull her up just as the second place filly strode past her. Baroness watched as the horse opened up to a length's lead, then another as the finish line glared ahead. She could hear the booming of hooves behind her closing fast, but instead of letting them advance, the gray filly ignored her rider and continued her run.

"It doesn't hurt," she told herself. "I can keep going. I'll be brave, I've earned this title."

With all that was left in her, she yanked her head from the grapple of her rider's hands, and increased her stride. She was pulling up short on one side, and knew she could not sustain her speed for very long, but she had to believe she could catch the horse in front of her. Taking a few strenuous steps, she found herself shoulder to shoulder with her opponent. Baroness refused to look at her, refused to acknowledge that there was any horse who could stop her from winning, because she had more desire to win than all of them.

Panting with fatigue, the filly beside her challenged only once as they neared the finish. Her jockey was whipping her, commanding her to pass Baroness, and she did for just an instant. Then she fell back a half-stride and Baroness persevered.

It was her left leg that crossed the finish line first. As her hoof touched the ground, applause erupted all around her. At that moment, the injured grey thoroughbred could feel nothing but happiness. The title of the Oaks was now hers.

She was pulled up immediately, and Tiffany was the first one at her side. Taking hold of one rein, she kissed the breathless filly over and over on the end of her nose.

"Thank you, Baroness," she said, her voice thick with emotion. "Thank you for trying so hard when you did not have to."

Baroness bobbed her head up and down, and she knew by the way Tiffany's eyes were shining as she looked back at her, that she was thanking her for all the love they had shared together. They would be friends forever.

Epilogue

BARONESS RETURNED TO THE STABLE that evening escorted only by Tiffany. She had left behind the crowds of well wishers, newspaper reporters, and photographers for the peace and solitude of her familiar stall. It mattered little to either the filly or the girl that Baroness was now what they called famous. They both understood that the real victory came in the form of the care and the confidence that the two friends had so freely given to each other.

The grey filly was limping from the strained tendon in her left foreleg, and she would certainly be more lame the next morning. Still, the veterinarian said that with proper attention and enough time off from training, it would surely heal. Whether Baroness would ever be able to race again would be in question for the many months to come, but whatever happened, Baroness knew that she and Tiffany would face it together.

Word of her victory at the Oaks did indeed find its way to the farm in Kentucky where her parents lived. It was Patches who first brought Freddie and Rosie the news.

Early that morning, the calico crawled into the lap of the farm owner and waited patiently for him to open the newspaper. Of course, since she was a cat, she could not read the words printed in it, but she could unquestionably make out the picture of the grey filly standing in the winner's circle.

151

Touching her paw to it, she mewed happily then scurried outdoors to tell her friends.

By her very appearance, Freddie knew that there was something to celebrate because she had a skip to her step and her long tricolored tail was pointed up merrily behind her. The chestnut stallion stood with Rosie and Woodrow, waiting expectantly for her to speak, and when she leaped up onto the fence the happiness in her eyes said everything.

"She won!" Patches declared jubilantly. "Baroness won the Oaks."

Freddie turned to Rosie and nuzzled her on the cheek. "Did you hear that, Rosie? Our daughter is a champion!"

Rosie returned his affection, and her lips curled into a knowing smile.

"Of course she is, Freddie," she answered sweetly. "She did not have to become famous for me to know that. We would be proud of her no matter what she had done."

"I couldn't have said it better myself," Woodrow barked.

It was already afternoon across the ocean in Ireland, and Baroness munched her hay as she looked out at the sloping emerald hills that were now her home. Freddie and Rosie had been in her thoughts often that day, and she wondered if they had heard of her win. Little could she know that on the other side of the world, where it was still very early, the lumber was being delivered to the farm where they lived. And on the abandoned foundation that had once been Royal Exile's barn, carpenters were hammering nails into the wood frame that was soon to be Freddie and Rosie's new home.

The spirit of true champions carries on forever.